Mystical Adventure of Ashley Sprinkler

SHERLINA IDID

Published by: Shariffah Norazlina Idid

Illustrations by Miblart

Edited by Teaspoon Publishing

ISBN: 9798535333434

To my family

Thanks for believing in me

CONTENTS

PROLOGUE

Thunder crashed and lightning flashed. A blue and green cyclone flashing with stardust approached Professor Sprinkler's laboratory that was hidden within the walls of his study.

The Professor was in the technology laboratory, in the midst of finalising his latest invention.

Tremors shook the bookshelves, and the drawers started to open and close frantically.

"Oh my! What's happening!" said Professor Sprinkler. He fled from the study to save his life, family, and his invention...

CHAPTER 1

STARTING A NEW LIFE

"Hooraayyy… Off we go in the plane," said Ashley.

When Ashley turned nine, her family had made plans to move into her grandmother's cottage in Kuala Lumpur as her grandmother was growing older and required someone to stay with her.

Nine-year-old Ashley, who had shoulder-length wavy brown hair and almond brown eyes, had unique features—her father originated from England and her mother was from Malaysia. Ashley was excited about the plan to live with her grandmother as she had a good bond with her grandmother as the only girl grandchild. Furthermore, she liked the cosy, ample space of her grandmother's cottage. She also liked to play in the garden with her grandmother's neighbour's cats and rabbit.

Ashley's father, Professor Sprinkler, was excited to continue working on his invention in his late father-in-law's laboratory as well as being a Senior Professor attached to an international research company. He was 182 cm tall and had slightly wavy light brown hair and almond brown eyes. He had huge black glasses and usually wore a grey shirt with two pockets located on the left and right of his chest.

The day scheduled for them to live with grandmother arrived. Upon reaching the cottage, Ashley quickly took her luggage and backpack from the car boot and ran into the cottage.

"Grandma...I missed you!" she cried out loudly. She hugged and kissed her grandmother upon seeing her at the entrance.

Without delay, she ran to the door towards the garden.

"Dash! Bob! Billy! Where are you?" cried out Ashley loudly.

She heard the bushes rustling and the trio appeared. The first cat, Dash, was golden-brown with brown stripes, while the other, a mocha-coloured cat with sapphire eyes, was named Bob. The rabbit, who had white fur and spotted brown ears, was named Billy.

"There you are," said Ashley as she hugged them.

CHAPTER 2

THE BEGINNING

One sunny day, Dash, Bob, and Billy went to play in Ashley's garden. Colourful butterflies flew around them as the trio played catch.

Suddenly, there was thunder and lightning and a heavy downpour started...*splish spash splash!*

Since it was too sudden, they did not manage to return home. Dash, Bob, and Billy ran for shelter under a rundown antique chair. Out of the blue, the trio saw a magical light flickering. Curious, they followed the magical purple and pink light that was shining on the brick wall...without realising it, they entered to another dimension.

"WOAHHHHHHHHH!" said Dash and Bob and Billy, "we are flying! Arrrgghhhhhhhhhhh!"

Suddenly, they felt that they were falling down.

Zoom!

"Whooaaaa what…"

Thud thud thud.

"Hold on tightly, guys…"

The trio were momentarily knocked out…

A gusty wind woke them.

"Where are we?" asked Dash.

There were so many passers-by…cars, buses, and motorcycles.

"This doesn't look like our backyard at all!" the trio exclaimed.

They bumped into a lady statue riding a horse. Dash read the label: *Lady Godiva of Coventry (Priory Street).*

"Good day, my lady," they said with a bow.

Dash, Bob, and Billy were well-trained and good-mannered. They smiled and talked to the statue. Unaware that it was not human, the trio were dismayed that the statue didn't respond to them.

So they walked and walked through bushes and pavement, wondering where they had landed.

Then they heard someone on the opposite pavement shouting, "SALE…Great SALE! Two pounds for a photo and three pounds for a scarf! Come and get it before it's gone…"

The trio stood and stared at the antics of the seller (who was wearing ugly, worn boots and had an apron-like cloth set on his pants). They were so amazed that they didn't realise that there was a ten-year-old blonde girl named Valerie about to catch all of them.

Kaaboommm!

"I got them…all three of them…they are going to be mine. They are so cute," Valerie said to herself.

The exasperated trio tried to escape from the little girl's clutches in vain. She placed them in a gunny sack, tied it tight, and placed it on her toy trolley. She covered the gunny sack with a torn blanket. The route to her cottage was rough as she passed through a muddy, pebbled path. It was a bumpy ride for the trio. They kept banging into each other as the space in the sack was limited.

Once they arrived, Valerie dashed upstairs into her room and opened the sack. The trio found themselves in an old English cottage. They could smell something cooking that made their tummies rumble.

The trio asked the little girl, "Where are we?"

Valerie peeped at them with her emerald eyes. She had pointed ears and the ability to understand animals. She replied, "Coventry, England, of course. HAHAHAHAHA…"

Dash asked, "What is your name, cute little girl, and what do you want from us?"

"You can call me Val," she replied. Val quickly placed them in a rusty cage on top of a wooden table. "SSSHHH keep quiet. Don't let Mother Reddy hear you, otherwise she will keep you for herself."

"Why does your mum want us for herself?" Dash asked.

Val was about to reply when…

"VALLLL!!" her mum shouted. "Come down for dinner."

Val quickly left her room.

This was the trio's chance to escape. They looked around for a sharp object to open the rusty cage to no avail.

Downstairs, Mother Reddy was holding a small heart-shaped crystal in her thin, pointy hands. She was a skinny woman with shoulder-length curly black hair.

"Gotcha…" she said. "Little girl, are you hiding something from mummy? I can see cat fur… ehmmm…rabbit fur…ehmmm…a fresh smell. It is good for me. Where did you hide them, Val? You better show them to me instantly." Mother Reddy shook Val by the shoulders until Val felt dizzy.

"SSHHHH!" Val said to her mother. "I have a surprise for you."

Val took Mother Reddy's hand and pulled her to her room. Mother Reddy opened the door and to her happiness, she saw the most precious ingredients she had been looking for—cat and rabbit fur, fresh and real.

Her eyes filled with creepy happiness. "Val, you just made your mum proud of you." She winked at Val. "I will make you your favourite chicken raspberry pie."

Tiptoeing quietly, Mother Reddy opened the door to the cage and grabbed Dash and Bob. She snipped their fur with her golden scissors, then placed both cats back into the cage. Next, she grabbed Billy and snipped his fur as well.

"That should do for the moment," Mother Reddy said to Val, "please ensure you feed and take good care of them. I will need to get more of their fur for my second experiment."

***

Ting Tong Ting! The clock chimed midnight.

Mother Reddy walked into her study. She pushed the antique clock on the side cupboard to the left and a hidden door slid open. She entered her Special Room, where she kept all kinds of spells and gadgets.

She talked to herself loudly. "This fur will make my potion complete…" She started to make the potion, mixing this and that, splashing here and there, singing and muttering spells whilst she was at it.

Finally, she put Dash's, Bob's, and Billy's fur into a huge crystal bowl. She started muttering her spell…then KABOOMMM…it turned into a smelly black rat.

"No! No! No! I got the spell wrong. ARGHHHH…" Mother Reddy cried aloud. Her face was blanketed with black smoke and slime that smelt like a dead rat.

Mother Reddy ran to the secret sliding door and shouted, "VAL…VAL!"

At her mother's shout, Val startled and jumped out from her single bed. She had already bid goodnight to the trio and turned off the lights. They heard heavy footsteps running up the stairs.

Mother stood at the foot of the stairs and shouted at Val. "Go and get more fur for me...I need to create the potion correctly this time!!!"

Whilst Val was talking to Mother Reddy at the top of the staircase, Billy tried his best to bite through the rusty cage door. Concurrently, Dash managed to get a sharp pin from beside the cage and they pushed the latch until it finally opened. The trio climb onto the windowsill beside the table and the girl's bed. They pushed hard at the window. Arggghhhhh! Billy accidentally hit the table lamp and it fell with a loud crash.

Mother Reddy and Val heard the commotion and ran into Val's room. They saw the window ajar. Mother Reddy quickly closed it. She took heavy bricks and stacked them against the window to prevent the trio from escaping. Then they grabbed the trio. The trio struggled but were unable to escape from their firm grips.

Mother Reddy and Val relocated the cage onto the floor beside Val's bed then pushed the trio in. Val replaced the latch with a brand-new brass padlock.

Val went back to sleep while her mother cleaned her Special Room.

***

As the clock chimed five in the morning, the trio whispered to each other. They were planning their second escape attempt.

The plan started with Billy biting the padlock whilst Dash and Bob gnawed on the wires of the cage but they failed to break out. Feeling frustrated, they stopped what they were doing and tried to think of another plan. The padlock could only be opened by a small key that Val had hidden in her nightgown pocket.

"Paper clip!" whispered Billy. "There is a paperclip lying on the floor, let's try to grab it. Dash, since you are the longest, reach out one of your paws for the paperclip. This is our only chance to escape."

Dash tried stretching out his paw. "Eeehhhharrrghhhh…oh my, this is tiring. I will try again…" After several attempts, he was finally able to reach the paperclip. Slowly, he cupped it and slid the paperclip into the cage.

"Gotcha!" said Dash. "Billy, since you are the heaviest amongst us, please step on the paperclip and break it in the middle."

Once the paperclip was broken, both cats used their sharp teeth to pull the paperclip into an 'L' shape. Then they inserted the L-shaped paper clip into the padlock and gave it a twist.

Click!

Val turned and opened one of her eyes to check on the trio. The trio held their breaths. They didn't dare to move a muscle. Val resumed her sleep.

A few minutes later, once they were confident that Val had fallen back into a deep sleep, Dash quietly opened the rusty cage door. Dash, Bob, and Billy crept to the bedroom door since the window was closed. Luckily for them, the door was not locked so they quickly tiptoed out of the room and down the stairs.

Upon reaching the ground floor, they found to their amazement that all the furniture was floating in the air as well as twirling up and down. In order to remain silent, they had to ensure that they didn't knock into any of the furniture.

They went from the living room to the dining room and out to the entrance hallway but, to their dismay, they were unable to find any door to escape. So they decided to enter the kitchen. The kitchen door creaked open. They were glad to see a window had been left slightly ajar—it had a weird shape that was asymmetrical in comparison to the other locked windows beside it.

Together, the trio pushed on the window until it finally budged open wide enough for them to fit. Without any hesitation, they jumped through the window and made their escape.

"Where shall we go?" Billy asked. "Which direction?"

Dash and Bob sniffed and pointed to the right. They had to find the magical gateway to return home and to do that, they had to return to where they had originally landed: Priory Street. They decided to head to the bus station on Priory Street as that would be a good place to hide in whilst waiting for the magical gateway to appear.

***

Val suddenly woke from her sleep. She glanced at the cage and, to her surprise, the cage door was ajar and the trio was missing. Upon seeing this, Val jumped out of bed, grabbed her sweater, and slipped on her pink glitter shoes. She planned to search for them so she ran downstairs.

"Val, is that you?" asked Mother Reddy, hearing her footsteps.

"The trio escaped, mum, so let me check the CCTV," Val said. She went to the TV panel on the side table in the living room. "Oh my," exclaimed Val, "I am unable to see them via the CCTV. They must have gone a distance."

"WHAT!" her mother screamed. "Go quickly and catch them…you must get them alive. I need them for my potion experiments."

Val unlocked the front door. With the help of her pink glitter shoes, Val was able to walk faster than a normal human. Val had also been born with a pointed nose that had a strong sense of smell. This helped her to search for the trio. She was able to catch their scent easily and tail them in the right direction.

With their strong sense of smell and vision, Dash, Bob, and Billy had managed to hop and walk through mud and bushes.

"Taaadaaaa," Val said as she tried to grab the trio.

The trio frantically scampered away and hid within the bushes. To Val's dismay, she did not manage to grab any of them.

"You better come with me, my cute friends. I have delicious carrots for the rabbit and fresh tuna fish for the cats," Val said loudly. "I promise I will take good care of you like my pets."

The air was suddenly still. Val put her hands into her pyjamas pocket and pulled out a shining pebble. The trio ran past her and she quickly threw the magic pebble in their direction. Smoke appeared and blanketed their vision.

"Oh my! I can't see!" yelled Billy.

They held each other's hands and walked cautiously through the smoke. *Splat!* Their paws sunk into the muddy sand. Val was able to see clearly into the thick smoke with her shining emerald eyes. She quickened her steps to grab them.

Billy saw bushes ahead. He grabbed Dash and Bob by their paws and pulled them into the bushes to hide from the smoke. Once they were no longer within the smoky spell's diameter, Val was unable to see them.

The trio noticed Val desperately searching for them in the opposite direction. They ran past cars and buses, and finally reached Priory Street. They took cover in the Pool Meadow Bus Station's janitor room and fell asleep.

After sleeping for five hours, Dash and Billy woke up and rubbed their eyes when the sun's rays seeped through the door frame. Bob was still fast asleep. A few minutes later, they saw a pale hand reaching through the door. Val had found them!

Billy and Dash grabbed Bob. They ran and hopped away through the busy street and emerged near Priory Hall.

There were many students lying on the grass, laughing and talking amongst themselves at the foot of the Coventry Cathedral.

Passers-by exclaimed, "Look at those two cute cats and that fat, fluffy rabbit!'

Billy looked angry at this remark. "Ish! I am cute and handsome too, you know," he said grumpily.

Val grabbed Billy whilst he was busy talking to himself. "GOT you, hooray!"

Suddenly, the sunny weather turned dark with thunder and lightning. A strong, gusty wind blew and the magical light appeared in front of the cathedral.

"Dash, look! There...let's go into it to go home," Bob said. The two cats scampered into the magical light.

"WOAHHHHHHHHH," said Dash and Bob, "we are flying arrrgghhhhhhhhhhhh!"

Sadness enveloped both their hearts, thinking of the rabbit's ill-fate at being left behind with Val.

CHAPTER 3

CLUELESS

"Ashley! Ashley! Where are you?"

"Mummy, I am here," said Ashley.

"Grandma's friend Aunty Caroline and her grandson David are here. Please shake their hands," said Mum. "Ashley, kindly bring David to play in our garden."

"Come on!" exclaimed Ashley. "Let's play on the swing." Off she went, smiling to herself.

"Let me push you," David said to Ashley. "OK let's take turns…"

The blue swing swung up and down.

"Let's play hide and seek…" David said.

Ashley ran and hid in one of the butterfly flower bushes with Delphinium flowers at the back of the garden.

"One, two, three, four, five, six, seven, eight! A lion is coming to get you," David said, giggling. He searched for Ashley from one butterfly flower bush to another. He walked past the Delphiniums near the blue swing. Stepping further, he said, "I am coming Ashley…"

Thud! Plonk!

"OUCH!" said David. "What was that?"

Two cats had fallen on David and all three scrambled on the ground. Upon hearing the commotion, Ashley ran in David's direction.

Ashley exclaimed, "Dash! Bob!" She picked them up and hugged them as they shivered and looked scared.

Meow! Meow! they said.

The two cats struggled to be freed from Ashley's arms, trying to tell her, "We have to save Billy."

After lots of meowing and paws pointing at the bushes, Ashley finally guessed the cats' request. She followed them towards the bushes. However, the magic path did not appear.

The cats tried to go through the wall but ended up having bruises on their foreheads.

Feeling hopeless and down, they went back next door.

CHAPTER 4

DEPARTURE

Whilst Ashley was in school the next day, Dash and Bob came to the cottage garden in search of the magical gateway. They tried pushing each brick of the garden wall with their paws, trying their luck to find an opening. However, there was none.

In the cottage upstairs, Professor Sprinkler was in Ashley's late grandfather's study, going through his diaries of past scientific findings. Professor Augustine's findings were experimental; some were successes and some were failures.

Nineteen years ago, both Professors were well-known researchers with the desire to invent new or improvise magical items with digital elements. Professor Sprinkler had been Professor Augustine's assistant, and they developed a good working friendship. Professor Sprinkler often visited his mentor's cottage, which was how he met and fell in love with Ashley's mother.

After their marriage, it took eight years for Ashley's mother to conceive a child. At the same time, Professor Sprinkler had been offered a lucrative Head of Research job in England, which led them to stay in England for nine years.

Beep…beep.

Professor Sprinkler heard a sound coming from the walls of the study. Curious, he tried to follow the direction of the sound. Since he was well-versed with the surroundings of the study, he got up from the chair and walked from one bookshelf to another. He stopped momentarily when the sound stopped.

Once he started to sit, however, the beeping sound resumed. *Beep…Beep…*

Professor Sprinkler headed towards the beeping. Using his special power of being able to see through objects, he was surprised to see a laboratory hidden within the walls of the study. He pushed the wall and it slid open. He entered the laboratory and was bewildered by the items in it. He started to locate the sound. As it turned out, the beeping was coming from a travel machine invention that he needed to complete as indicated in the diary left by Professor Augustine.

Soon, Professor Sprinkler was so deeply involved with his inventions that he seldom came out from the study to spend time with his family.

"The invention, energy, and the greed of 'beings' from different realms has caused lots of unrest and negative consequences to me. I need to ensure that Ashley is well prepared when I am gone," said Professor Sprinkler to himself.

***

Several months passed and Ashley seemed to be adapting well to the new school environment and culture. She was attending a school near to her grandmother's cottage and had managed to make friends with two girls, Melissa and Sheila.

One day whilst Ashley was in school, Professor Sprinkler was in the study when a cyclone from another dimension managed to enter Earth's dimension. In order to save his life, Professor Sprinkler jumped into his car and drove at a high speed, causing it to skid.

An hour before school ended, her teacher called her out of the class. "Please come to the counselling room with me, Ashley," she said.

Ashley looked surprised. She got up from her chair and followed her teacher to the room.

The class teacher said, "Ashley, please sit down. I am sorry to inform you of some bad news. Your beloved father has just died in a car crash."

Tears fell from Ashley's almond brown eyes. Her teacher comforted her by hugging her and kissing her forehead. She took out a box of tissues for Ashley to wipe her tears. At the same time, she spoke to her in a soothing tone of encouragement.

"I would like to give you a word of encouragement for you to be strong. It is our mind that controls our well-being, to be strong, happy, or sad," said the teacher. "I encourage you to be positive and strong at heart, so that you can protect your mother and grandmother once you grow older. You will survive while maintaining a strong bond with your family."

***

A week after the funeral, Ashley went to her father's study to take his folder of bills and letters for her mother. In the midst of searching for it, Ashley tripped and fell onto the dark blue Persian carpet, knocking some photo frames askew.

"Ouch!" she exclaimed.

Suddenly, Ashley heard a sound coming from the wall behind her grandfather's and father's tilted photo frames.

"What on earth?"

A small space appeared in the concrete wall. Curious, Ashley pushed her father's chair against the wall and climbed on it to investigate.

She heard footsteps and quickly straightened the frame. She pushed the chair back to its place and pretended to search for Dad's folder. Mum came into the room and saw the photo frame. She started crying as she missed her late husband.

"Ashley," Mum said, "please search quickly for the folder and give it to me in my room."

"Yes, mum…" Ashley opened the chest of drawers at the desk. "Found it, mum!" she exclaimed loudly and proudly.

***

The next day, as Ashley was in the garden playing on the swing, the two cats came out from the butterfly flower bushes. *Meow Meow,* they tried talking to Ashley but she could not understand them. She wondered why the cats were running frantically around the bushes.

Then Ashley asked, "Is your rabbit friend sick since he is not with you today?"

"Meow!" said Dash and Bob sadly.

The two cats were trying their best to find the magical gateway to save their rabbit friend. They spent their time in Ashley's garden chasing butterflies and running around. Ashley was playing on the blue swing when the weather changed. The sky turned dark, with thunder and lightning. From afar, a magical light appeared but this time it was blue and purple.

The cats' fur stood on end, a puff of erect fur forming at the base of their tails. Ashley's hair and her top swayed in the direction of the magical gateway.

"Wobbly rockets! Wwwhat iiinn the wworld is hhaaapppening?" said Ashley.

Unable to withstand the strong wind, the three of them were sucked into the magical gateway. In the gateway, they could see sparkling blue and purple lights.

CHAPTER 5

SURPRISE

Ashley, Dash, and Bob were awakened by the sound of birds chirping. They found themselves lying on a bed of bluebells.

Ashley groaned and opened her eyes wide when she suddenly remembered her journey. "Cats! Where are you?"

A few feet from her, she saw the two furry cats.

"Where are we?" Ashley asked, grabbing the two cats.

The two cats were surprised to find themselves in an enchanted forest. There were crooked trees with purple coral bells and bluestar flowers surrounding them. Whilst looking around, they spotted a cloud of shining colourful dust straight ahead. It was like magic forced their feet to walk following the shining colourful dust.

After an hour of walking, Ashley felt dismayed and puzzled.

"Wait…didn't we walk here twenty minutes ago?" Ashley asked.

The trees looked the same, surrounded by delphinium bushes. Cherry-scented smoke blinded their vision. Their legs kept on walking straight on the path, which was lined with purple coral bells and bluestar flowers. They walked past a river which had symmetrical shades of blue, which encompassed azure blue on its furthest left, maya blue in the centre, and turquoise on its right. There was sprinkle of shining dust on top of it, making it look magical.

Ashley and the cats stopped walking at the end of the river and looked around. They were surrounded by a forest of crooked trees with purple and blue flowers and mint leaves. The magical smoke in front of their eyes cleared, forming into a cloud-like staircase. Ashley and the cats climbed the cloud staircase for thirty minutes. Whilst climbing, they caught a glimpse of the overall enchanted forest which was in the shape of diamond.

At the top of the clouds, an enchanted garden with red fern leaves and turquoise Delphinium flowers lay before them.

"This is like a dream. Where are we?" exclaimed Ashley.

The two cats quivered and hugged each other. They felt that there was something fishy about this place once their paws touched the ground.

The square garden they landed in was a maze. It was a large, well-maintained knot filled with plants and four-season hydrangeas, such as oakleaf, smooth, panicle, and beautiful bigleaf hydrangeas. Fernleaf bleeding heart flowers were also scattered everywhere.

They walk through the garden until they panted due to dehydration. They stopped momentarily to catch their breath.

Both cats meowed, "This is too far. Where are we?"

Ashley's eyes widened with bewilderment. "Unbelievable! I can understand you, Dash and Bob," she said in surprise.

Ashley carried the cats in her arms as they looked lethargic. "Let's find water and place to rest," she said while patting them.

As Ashley walked past red ferns and beautiful bigleaf hydrangeas, she felt a sprinkle of water on her sleeve. She smiled to herself. They were finally approaching a source of water to drink and a place to rest. Ashley made a left turn and saw a large water garden. In the midst of the ponds, there was a diamond-shaped pond with a fountain.

They walked towards the fountain. However, they were unable to reach it as the thick garden maze bushes led them to a dead end.

They retraced their steps and tried walking in the opposite direction, hoping to find an open path to the fountain. As they were approaching the fountain, it suddenly disappeared in front of their eyes. Ashley placed both cats on the ground. Dash and Bob ran on ahead, continuing in the initial direction of the fountain. There was a loud bang.

"Ouch!" said Dash and Bob simultaneously.

"There is something blocking our pathway here," said Dash.

When Ashley reached the site of the fountain, she said, "Dear Sir or Madam, we have been travelling so far and we are thirsty. We would appreciate if you could allow us to drink water from your fountain."

Suddenly, the fountain became visible before their eyes.

"Wow! That is cool, Ashley! We do need to have permission to drink," meowed Dash.

Dash was so impatient that he pushed Bob aside in order to be the first one to drink the water. He drank greedily from the diamond-shaped pond.

Ashley and Bob gasped in surprise, freezing as Dash turned into a statue made of opals. The weather suddenly changed. A fast wind blew in a twisting and turning pattern.

"Look...look the magical light has appeared. Let's hold on to Dash so we can bring him home and get help," said Ashley.

Unfortunately, the statue was not taken by the magical light forces. Only Ashley and Bob were pulled by its powerful current into the magical gateway even though both of them tried to pull Dash along with them.

This time, the path was navy blue with lightning-like swirls that knocked Ashley and Bob out.

Dosshhhh....

Ashley and Bob fell onto the butterfly flower bush outside Ashley's grandmother's cottage. It felt as though they had been away for months on the journey. Both felt relieved to return home.

Lightning and thunder sounded amidst a heavy downpour...*splish spash splash.*

Magical lights appeared and off they went again...

CHAPTER 6

GUINEA PIG

In Coventry, Val had managed to grab Billy. She returned to her cottage in the quiet neighbourhood of Coundonny Don.

"You little brat. How could your friends escape from me!"

Mother Reddy heard Val's footsteps. "Val, come and give me the animals. What, you only have the rabbit! What happened to the two cats? Never mind I will make my magic using the rabbit first. Give me the rabbit."

Billy shivered. He was so afraid of what would happen to him, living with these two people.

Mother Reddy took the rabbit from Val and walked into her Special Room.

"Don't worry, my cute furry friend. I am just going to use your beautiful fur for my experiment," Mother Reddy said. "Then I will release you."

Mother Reddy snipped the rabbit's spotted fur. She was experimenting with animal fur to increase the efficiency of her potion. She placed the fur into a crystal bowl along with other ingredients. WOOOSHHHHHHH....

"My magic is alive! Hahahhahaahhaaha! My potion better be perfect this time, I need to unfreeze a valuable item in the enchanted garden castle soon," she said out loud.

Billy saw her greedy eyes and shivered in fear.

"Kalooalakaloo...my beautiful potion...mixed with this, mixed with that! Some rabbit fur in my potion...allaalaakalooalakaloo." Mother Reddy twirled and danced away happily in front of her potion experiment, confident that she finally had the right ingredients. "Let me try this on you, rabbit... hahahahahaa...you will be my guinea pig... hahahaahahaha! Did I say pig?" She snorted and laughed loudly.

Mother Reddy grabbed the rabbit from the cage, placed him on a dentist's chair and fastened the belt to ensure the rabbit stayed still. Billy struggled to escape from her strong grip but failed.

"Don't worry, my furry little friend. I am only going to make your furry legs disappear. Hahahaha." Mother noticed the rabbit tearing up in fear. "Oh my, my! What I mean is you'll still have your legs but they will be invisible…hahahahaaha."

Mother sprinkled some magic potion onto Billy's legs. In a split second, his legs were invisible.

"Do you still feel your legs, my dear furry friend?" asked Mother Reddy.

Billy tested by wriggling his toes and moving his legs. He felt them alright, although he was unable to see them. He nodded.

Mother Reddy said, "My magic potion is finally successful! Yes!" She danced a little on the spot. "Let me try to undo this spell. Booblllueebrrr!"

Billy's legs were still invisible.

"Oh my. I am sorry, my furry friend. Let me put you into the cage while I check my ancient spell book for how to reverse the spell. I am not getting younger, you know. Where did I keep the ancient spell book? Let me see…"

She placed her right hand into the empty space just above her forehead and took out a red vase.

Mother Reddy exclaimed, "No, no, no, this is not the one."

She slipped her right hand into another empty space and pulled out a duck feather. Patiently, she slipped her hand into each next empty space. It was the fifteenth space when she finally pulled out a rectangular object.

"Aah, I found it! But what is the password? Let me try this..."

Tid! She'd entered the wrong password!

"Let me reset the password."

Finally, Mother Reddy was able to access the ancient spell book. She quickly turned the pages.

"Nope, this is not the one..." Mother Reddy flipped to the next page and the next...

She sighed and dropped the ancient spell book on the table. The drawer of the table suddenly opened. An electronic dictionary flew in her direction. When she touched it with her fingerprint, the electronic device opened.

"*The spell to undo invisibility chapter 1002*—the main ingredient can only be found within Desperate Valley," Mother Reddy read. "Val!" she screamed. She quickly went upstairs to find that Val was fast asleep.

***

When the sun rose, Mother Reddy woke Val up and told her that they were going on an adventure. Val's emerald eyes widened with excitement.

"This will be treacherous journey," Mother Reddy said.

Immediately, Val knew that she had to equip herself by wearing her pink glitter shoes and tying her hair with a magical rubber band. She also put some magic dust in a brown leather pouch that she strapped around her waist.

Mother Reddy wore her hooded dark blue cloak and brought some magic dust. She also packed her magic wand, which looked like a twisted branch adorned with small roses in metallic gold.

They walked to the garden at the back of the cottage. The garden overlooked a messy wood with long grass. Mother Reddy pointed her magic wand towards the empty space in front of them and muttered a magic spell.

Immediately, the ground tremored, causing Mother Reddy and Val to nearly fall. However, they managed to balance themselves by holding each other's hands. Within a minute, a magic pathway opened for them.

A pungent smell of decay lingered in the atmosphere of the other realm. Mother Reddy and Val covered their noses as they entered the realm. Smoky clouds gathered above their heads. They kept walking, even though they struggled with poor visibility.

This realm was covered with trees with crooked branches with sharp olive-coloured leaves. There were no flowers. The path was muddy and filled with insects. Their shoes frequently sank in the muddy path which reduced their pace.

"We are to steal the Moment of Truth leaves," Mother Reddy told Val, "and one of the Three Weird Sisters' hairpins in order to undo the spell. Both can be found at the Weird Sisters' mansion in the deepest valley of the enchanted forest."

While walking, they bumped into four dangerous Tata Duende. All the Tata Duende looked alike: they were 92 cm tall and had pointy faces, flat noses, and hooded red eyes. They could only be told apart by the colour of their pointed hats. The ones Mother Reddy and Val faced now had two-toned pointed hats—basil and olive, coral and orange, and green and aquamarine.

"What is your prophecy?" the one who wore the coral and orange pointed hat asked in an eerie echo.

Mother Reddy replied, "We are the family of the Three Weird Sisters. We are here to visit."

The Tata Duende in the green and aquamarine hat said, "Show me your ID for proof. Otherwise, no entry beyond this corner."

"Let me show you my dark blue cloak as my ID," said Mother Reddy. She flashed and wiggled her blue cloak, expecting it to release smoke and blind the Tata Duende. However, her magic cloak was limited in its power in front of the Tata Duende. Nothing happened.

"You are an imposter. Entrance forbidden," said the Tata Duende in the green and aquamarine hat.

"Please let us in," Mother Reddy begged but to no avail.

The Tata Duende grew to a giant size, blocking the way.

Sadly, both retraced their journey and returned to the muddy ground full of long olive grasses.

Mother Reddy said, "We need a plan to snatch the stuff." She took out a blank sheet of paper from her cloak and started to strategise their entrance.

Day turned to night. It was very quiet in the Desperate Valley forest. Mother Reddy and Val started walking to the opposite end of the valley as their plan was to enter via the back of the valley. They walked and walked through the muddy ground and tall grass. Val's pink glitter shoes emitted a light that assisted their vision.

CHAPTER 7

BIRTHDAY PARTY

The Weird Sisters' mansion was brightly lit. The two-storey mansion's quaint design was a dull cream. It had been built 109 years ago and had ten rooms, including the kitchen. It was surrounded with crooked olive-coloured pine trees. The entrance was guarded by four fierce Tata Duende and a magic iron gate.

Three sisters lived in the mansion. Angie, the youngest, was a thin young lady who liked to wear dresses. Cindy was a middle-aged lady who loved to wear blue jeans. Danielle, the oldest, looked dashingly beautiful due to her two-toned sparkling peach and cream eyes and blue hair and was a fan of wearing baggy pants. They were known as the Three Weird Sisters. They possessed weird magic and potions from different realms for any kinds of situations.

It was Cindy's birthday and her two sisters were planning a surprise party. In order to make it a surprise, they asked Cindy to collect some crooked branches from Desperate Valley's enchanted forest for their latest invention spell.

"Do come back before nightfall as I am cooking your favourite soup," said Angie, the best cook in the family.

Once Cindy left the mansion, the two sisters happily transformed the guest room into a nicely decorated hall with pink, golden, and lilac-coloured artificial roses. Party balloons were twisted into an arch over the entrance to the room. They hung balloons on each chair. The long dining table in the centre of the room was lit with candles from the ancient days.

In the kitchen, Angie was busy cooking a feast. She made snails and oxtail soup, turkey, and salad. She also baked a two-tiered birthday cake with jelly for dessert.

The sun was starting to set by the time Cindy collected enough crooked branches in her backpack. She started to walk back to the mansion. Whilst walking, she smelt two unidentified creatures in the enchanted forest. Cindy was born with a magic nose which was hypersensitive to the slightest change of smell in the air. She stopped and sniffed.

Who are these intruders, she whispered in her heart. *Let me inform my sisters about this.*

Within ten minutes, she reached the mansion looking messy and tired.

"Aw, I am so tired," Cindy exclaimed to her two sisters. "I'll take a shower."

"Sure," Danielle said. "Please come down to have dinner with us as Angie has cooked your favourite soup."

Cindy went upstairs to her room in the west wing of the old mansion, still in deep thought about the smell of the two strange creatures. She quickly bathed and changed into her new colourful dress and a matching hair band that she bought online to wear on her birthday.

"Unbelievable!" she said to herself. "Both of my sisters didn't remember my birthday. They never wished me and instructed me to spend my birthday in the enchanted forest alone."

Feeling down, she went downstairs to the dining area. The dining room was in darkness so she used a finger spell to light the room. There was no food to be seen. However, possessing a magic nose, she could smell the delicious food in the guest room connected to the dining room. So she skipped and walked over, thinking happily of Angie's soup as she pushed the door open. To her surprise, confetti was thrown from the ceiling. Danielle and Angie sang 'Happy Birthday' to Cindy and, using their magic, brought in a live orchestra and a hologram of her favourite idol, J-Hope of BTS, to entertain them throughout the night.

CHAPTER 8

HOLD ON TO YOUR BREATH

Deep inside the enchanted forest, Mother Reddy and Val continued their journey. The sun had set and the enchanted forest was pitch dark. It was unusually quiet, without any sound of insects. Only their footsteps could be heard. As they approached the old mansion, Mother Reddy put up the hood of her cloak. Val walked closely while leaning against her mother's cloak to ensure no one was aware of them. One of the cloak's innate powers was to camouflage its wearers according to their surroundings. Mother Reddy did not want to use her magic wand as the Weird Sisters were able to sense if different magic was being used nearby. They jumped over the rusty, sharp gate that was covered with lots of small leaves. They heard loud music from inside the mansion.

"They are busy with a party," Mother Reddy said. "This will be our chance to sneak into the old mansion to grab those magical ingredients."

They were lucky to find that the kitchen window had been left slightly ajar. They jumped in through the window. When their feet touched the floor with a soft thud, an alarm triggered.

"Oh my God," Mother Reddy whispered.

The Weird Sisters stopped dancing and looked at each other.

"It must be an intruder!" they cried out loudly. In a flash, all three of them tiptoed towards the kitchen.

"I feel I am going to have my heart attack," whispered Mother Reddy. "Let's quickly hide at the back of the cupboard. It seems to be a good hiding place." They crept into the dark brown antique cupboard. In addition, Mother Reddy covered both herself and Val with her magic cloak.

Upon reaching the kitchen, the Weird Sisters opened the door with their magic fingers. They crept in and saw that the window was ajar. A gusty wind blew against their skin.

Angie said, "Oh my, I totally forgot to close the window after cooking."

They searched the whole kitchen thoroughly for any item or intruder that had triggered the alarm. With their sensitive noses and ears, they investigated, starting from the wash basin that was located just below the open window. Satisfied that there was no intruder there, they skimmed their senses and vision towards the three-tiered kitchen cabinet on the left of the basin. It was not disturbed, so they checked the last item in the kitchen— the antique cupboard.

It didn't look like the cupboard had been disturbed. Cindy sniffed it, coming near to their hiding spot. Mother Reddy and Val held their breaths and stood still. Luckily for them, the magic cloak protected them.

Unable to find anything, Danielle and Angie grabbed hold of Cindy's hands and went off. The three Weird Sisters went back to the guest room and continued eating, singing, and dancing.

***

Mother Reddy and Val quietly opened the kitchen door and crept out. The items had to be in one of the rooms and there were nine rooms to search!!

First, they went to a room in the east wing situated just above the kitchen. The room was decorated with family photos. They saw pictures of the Weird Sisters' parents, grandparents, and great-grandparents along with antique statues of their pets. They looked behind each of the ten pet statues on the long table. However, it was not there.

They went to the next room, where they found computers, scanners, and a printer. Mother Reddy quickly flipped through the piles of papers with her skinny old fingers. Feeling exasperated at not being able to find the magic ingredients after searching three rooms, Mother Reddy pointed for Val to leave the room.

Once they were outside overlooking the west wing of the mansion, they saw a wide Georgian spiral staircase. They walked quietly towards the staircase and climbed up. To their surprise, it led them to an empty space at the topmost level of the house. All around them were rows of shelves, an antique writing table, and an antique cupboard.

Mother Reddy and Val were about to tilt a table lamp and search for the Moment of Truth leaves and the magic hairpin when they heard footsteps. They froze.

"Let's hide," Mother Reddy said to Val.

Quickly, they hid in the antique cupboard. This time, the cupboard was so dusty they had to hold their breaths to prevent themselves from sneezing.

***

The clock had struck midnight and the Weird Sisters called it a day, returning to their bedrooms. Danielle pulled Cindy's sleeve and whispered for Cindy to follow her.

"I have something to give you," she said.

They climbed to the topmost level of the house.

"Cindy, Grandma Albae asked me to give you this magical hairpin on your hundredth birthday," Danielle said, holding out a golden hairpin. "This magical hairpin can do wonders. Its powerful magic can make an invisible item visible and vice versa. It can bring you to different dimensions and has the ability to transform you into anything. Of course, you need to utilise the power sensibly since it can destroy anyone or anything if not used correctly for the right purpose. The reason Grandma Albae gave this gift to you is because of the adventure in your blood."

Cindy was speechless as she pinned the golden hairpin in her hair.

Finally, at one in the morning, Danielle and Cindy went back to their bedrooms to sleep.

Mother Reddy and Val heard the conversation and knew that it was the item that they required. They had to go to Cindy's room to get the hairpin when she was asleep. They climbed down the stairs and they were lucky that the first room on the west wing was Cindy's room.

The door was unlocked. Mother Reddy saw the hairpin on the small bedside table. She tried to snatch it, but a powerful force froze her hands.

"So you are the one that I smelt in the enchanted forest," Cindy said. Cindy was aware of Mother Reddy's presence in her room since she has strong magical nose.

Val came to her mother's rescue. She blew magic dust towards her mother's hands, releasing her from the spell. In a flash, Mother Reddy grabbed the hairpin and stuck it in her black curls. They ran away as fast as they could.

Cindy was furious. She pointed her magic fingers in their direction to trap them in a spell, to no avail. Mother Reddy's cloak camouflaged them as they ran.

Awoken by the commotion, Danielle went to check out the situation. When she saw Cindy's magic fingers aiming at a fast-moving blur, she realised that there was an intruder in the old mansion. Without hesitation, Danielle pointed her magic fingers in the cloak's direction.

Kaboommm!

Mother Reddy and Val immediately stopped. A watery potion soaked the cloak and prevented the cloak's magic from working. Trembling with fear, Val took out her magic dust and blew it onto Mother Reddy and herself. However, the magic dust only managed to cover herself.

Mother Reddy was caught in Danielle's magic. She struggled to move but she was unable to do so. Before she was paralysed fully, she managed to throw her magic wand towards Val.

"Run, Val! Save yourself!"

Val caught the wand and ran away. Her pink glitter shoes transported her to the edge of the enchanted forest. Using her mother's magic wand, a magic pathway opened and Val quickly walked through it, thick clouds blinding her.

This time the scene and air smelt different. *Sniff…sniff…* Val tried to identify where she was.

CHAPTER 9

THE GIFT

Ashley and Bob trembled with fear at Dash's fate.

"Ashley, go clean yourself up and let's have dinner together," Ashley's mother called.

"Let's meet up every day to search for the magical gateway," said Ashley to Bob before he sadly returned to his house.

At the dining table with Mum and Grandma, Ashley started talking about her adventure at the enchanted forest.

"Your dad used to tell me about his adventure trips in an enchanted forest. However, I could not comprehend how he got there," Grandma said. "Your granddad and dad would like you to own everything in his study. He did mention that you would like the 'experience' of a lifetime."

Ashley smiled, nodded at Grandma, and started imagining what Dad had meant by 'experience of a lifetime'.

The morning sunlight crept into Ashley's window and woke her up.

Ashley was impatient. Once breakfast was over, she went to the garden to find Bob. She found him at the swing area and told him that she would bring him along for her adventure just in case it led to the magical gateway to save both Dash and Billy.

They walked upstairs and entered Dad's study. It was an elegant room with straight-backed comfortable wooden chairs and an antique writing table in mahogany brown. The expensive Persian carpet she had fallen on before had a peacock design. She placed Bob on the carpet as she looked for objects that would take her on an adventure. Her fingers lingered on her father's bookshelves full of leatherbound books with gold and silver writing. She tried to read each book's title...

"Is there anything on adventure that I could read?" she whispered to herself.

Bob sniffed here and there in the study, trying his best to find the magical gateway. Bob sniffed along the walls until he reached where the photo of Dad and Granddad hugging each other hung. The smell was familiar. He sniffed again. This time it was obvious. He stood up on his back paws to catch Ashley's attention.

"There is nothing on the wall except for the photo frame, Bob," Ashley said.

Bob sniffed again and Ashley pulled the wooden chair over for the cat to stand on it. He jumped onto the chair, sniffed the wall, and touched the frame. Ashley accidentally stepped onto something hard on the floor that was covered by the carpet. As she fell, the frame tilted and a small opening appeared on the cream-painted concrete wall.

Eyes wide, Ashley shifted Bob aside. She climbed onto the chair as she was not tall enough to reach the opening. The opening revealed a space like a safe box with a combination lock. Ashley tried her father's birthdate for the password but it didn't open. She tried her mother's birthday and then their anniversary date next but both numbers didn't work.

Ashley looked at Bob and said, "Let's ask Grandma. She should have the clue to the password."

Ashley grabbed Bob and ran towards the small tea room to find Grandma. True enough, Grandma was seated on her wooden rocking chair, sipping tea from British china teacup.

"Grandma, Grandma...please, please tell me a clue...I found an opening in Dad's study which requires a combination number."

Grandma's black eyes opened wide with surprised. "Come Ashley, please sit down beside Grandma. I remember late one night, I could not sleep. I heard a commotion and saw a blue flash of light from the study. Curious, I opened the door to the study and I saw your dad holding a small pocket book in green leather. He was trying to open something in the wall. I believe the password is kept there. It should be hidden in one of the drawers in the room."

Ashley thanked her grandmother and kissed her on the cheek. She took Bob and ran upstairs to Dad's study. She scanned the room and saw the bulky side table that Grandma had described beside the bookshelves. She went straight to the chest of drawers and found the small, green pocket book that Grandma mentioned. She opened the book. To her surprise, there was nothing in it. It was just an empty book, pages turning yellow as it aged.

Determined to find the password, she turned the pages of the book one by one in order not to miss any clue. Upon reaching the centre of the pocket book, a feather fell out. She picked up the feather. To her surprise, there was a combination of numbers and alphabets on it that looked like a top secret password. Without thinking, she immediately climbed the wooden chair, stood on it, and pressed the combination onto the keypad. The small space opened. Inside, there was a small box and a piece of paper.

To my lovely daughter Ashley,
When you came to my world, I knew deep inside my heart that adventure is in your blood.
With that I would like to present you the gift 'experience of a lifetime'.
Look no further. Flip open the box that looks like a book. The items inside are yours to keep.
There is always a way to return to the original. Persevere with the journey and be confident that you will succeed.
Love always,
Daddy

Ashley opened the pecan-coloured box made of hickory wood. She was awed to find a golden bracelet with two round charms inside. One of the charms was a plain circle while the other was a diamanté charm covered with blue, pink, and peach-coloured balls. There was also a ring with numbers on it. The numbers seemed to be moving automatically, like that of a digital watch. Ashley wore the bracelet on her right hand and placed the auto-ring on the middle finger of her left hand. Then she said out loud,

"Now what?" She shook the bracelet and played with the auto-ring. Nothing magical seemed to happen.

Feeling disappointed, Ashley went to bed early after dinner. She informed her mother that she would like Bob to sleep a night with her so that her mother could inform their neighbour.

CHAPTER 10
COVENTRY

Past midnight, strong, gusty winds started blowing. Lightning flashed and thunder sounded, followed by a heavy downpour. The numbers on Ashley's auto-ring started to spin crazily forwards and backwards. Concurrently, her bracelet charms started to glow. A clashing sound woke Bob up, who meowed in Ashley's ear until she woke up abruptly.

Bob pointed at the window with his paw. There was a flickering light near the garden wall and a magical gateway made of light appeared. Ashley and Bob quickly ran into the garden towards the light. They jumped into the magical light, which flashed a greyish black. They hugged each other and closed their eyes.

"Arghh! This is too fast!" said Ashley.

Boing…they landed on bushes and were covered with sand. Suddenly, Val came out from the direction of the overgrown forest.

"Urgh! Unbelievable! I landed at our filthy neighbour, Mr Spitstone's yard instead. Full of long grasses with dirty trash thrown here and there on the lawn," Val complained loudly.

Ashley grabbed Bob and hid behind the bushes.

Bob tried to tell Ashley that the girl was Val, the one who took Billy captive.

Ashley said, "Bob, oh my God, this is the second time that I understand each word you say to me. I noticed that I started to understand animal language when I embarked on these magical journeys. Or is it because of the scientific items that I am wearing now?"

Val was talking out loud to herself, while crying. "Unbelievable! Mother has been captured by the Three Weird Sisters of Desperate Valley. What should I do? I need to rescue Mother."

Val went straight to Mother Reddy's Special Room via the study. She pushed the antique clock located on the side cupboard and a hidden door slid open. Val was surprised to see many new potions, electronic gadgets, and a computer in the room.

"Rabbit!" she shouted. "There you are. Where is the invisible magic potion?"

Billy pointed in answer. Val turned her head towards a steel table. On it was a sparkling crystal bowl. Val placed her hands in the air just above her forehead and took out a red vase. She poured the invisible magic potion into the vase.

"Oh...this should do the trick." Without hesitation, she brought Billy along for the rescue mission.

Upon hearing what had happened to Mother Reddy, Ashley and Bob made plans to save Billy. After Val entered her cottage, Ashley and Bob also tried to enter the cottage via a window on the first floor that was slightly ajar.

First, they took a ladder that they found lying in the garden and placed it against the wall so that Ashley could climb in through the open window. Bob followed behind Ashley. Upon reaching the window, Ashley tried to push it wider for them to enter. Before entering, Ashley peeked through the gap between the windows to ensure that there was no one in the room.

"The coast is clear," she whispered to Bob. She entered by placing her head then her body into the room. She fell onto a bean bag as Bob climbed down from the window.

"Woah, what is this place?" Ashley's bracelet started glowing like a torch so that they could see in the darkness. "This looks like an attic," Ashley said.

There was a wooden trunk, an antique cupboard with lots of photos, and a rocking chair. Ashley went straight to the door with the intention to find the rabbit. When she touched the doorknob, a magic force gripped her hand, not allowing it to be released from the doorknob. Her right hand just remained still, unable to move a muscle.

Thinking quickly, Ashley moved her left hand, and pointed the auto-ring in the direction of the doorknob. She rubbed the auto-ring several times. A powerful green light shone from the ring towards the doorknob. In an instant, Ashley's hand and the doorknob were released. They stepped out of the room.

To their bewilderment, the first floor of the cottage was empty. Not a single piece of furniture could be seen. Ashley and Bob tiptoed to find another room to search for Billy, just in case he was being held captive.

Bob pulled Ashley closer and whispered, "The last time we were here, Mother Reddy had a special room for her magic experiments. We should find that room."

There were four rooms on the first floor. They opened the door to each room but the rooms looked normal, not like the 'special room' Bob remembered. As they opened the door of the fourth room, a colourful bird with a huge head and beak swung from the edge of one cupboard to the next. Ashley and Bob were confident that this fourth room was the Special Room, so they entered without realising that they were entering Mother Reddy's room. They had to duck every time the bird flew above their heads.

The room was full of magic. The antique marble chair was afloat; a toothbrush, toothpaste, and hairbrush also hung mid-air, as though they were lying on an invisible table. As they walked further into the room, they felt the uneven movement of the wooden floor.

They walked towards another door which opened by itself. A magic force pushed them into the small room. Suddenly Ashley and Bob were drenched as water magically dropped from the ceiling, filling the small room with bubbles. In a second, a bathing brush scrubbed Ashley's back as well as Bob's fur. Once the bathing activity was done, the magic force pushed Ashley and Bob out into the bedroom with towel over them. A huge dryer blew them both dry. Ashley and Bob ran towards the door. This was the wrong room, not the Special Room.

After checking all the rooms on the first floor, they decided to go downstairs. They headed towards the dining room and the living room but there was nothing peculiar there. Then they continued their search by heading to the kitchen. The kitchen was sparkling clean. All the cutlery were set neatly in glass cupboards. Suddenly, a door banged shut.

Ashley and Bob quietly opened the kitchen door and looked out but they didn't see anything. Bob started to sniff the floor and carpet to find a trace of Billy or Val. He sniffed for five minutes around the front door, going round and round until he stopped in front of the sofa in the living room. He stood up straight and pointed his paws at the study. Ashley and Bob ran into the study. To their dismay, the room looked peaceful. No rabbit or experiment was to be found. As they were about to walk out of the room, Ashley's bracelet moved, making a clashing sound. A strong energy pushed Ashley's right hand in the opposite direction.

"This must be where the Special Room is," exclaimed Ashley excitedly.

They walked towards the blank wall and scanned with their eyes for any clue on how to open the door. Bob started sniffing again. He could smell Mother Reddy's fingers on the antique clock in the side cupboard, so he pushed the clock with his back. A hidden door slid open.

They looked at each other with happiness. They had finally found the Special Room!

The Special Room was full of different smells due to the different potions and magic dust. As they stepped further into the room, they were bewildered to find the latest computer with other gadgets as well a wide screen in the middle of the room. As they walked in the direction of the computer, they felt a strong force pulling them away. They decided to follow the force to search for Billy.

In front of them was a shining crystal bowl with potion droplets on a wooden table. The table was messy with books, feathers, and rat fur. Bob resumed sniffing. He could identify Billy's smell on the dentist chair. Bob climbed onto the chair and continued sniffing then he jumped in the direction of an automatic cage.

***

Whilst Ashley and Bob walked into the kitchen to look for Billy and the Special Room, Val was taking Billy away via the front door of the cottage. Val equipped herself with her pink glitter shoes and magical hair tie. She brought additional magic dust in a brown leather pouch as well.

Val went to the back of the cottage garden and pointed her mother's magic wand at the empty space. She was expecting tremors again, however, this time she found herself on sandy land. She saw caves and mountains. Billy hugged her, trembling with fear.

"Oh my," Val cried out loudly, "the magic wand must have directed us to another realm!"

CHAPTER 11

THE GARDENS

Deep inside the Enchanted Gardens lived a friendly young prince who placed his citizen's needs as his priority.

Fifteen years ago, when Prince Jeff was born, the King and Queen of the Enchanted Gardens Realm, also known as the Goodness Realm, gave up their magic to be borne by their only son so he would be strong enough to protect the realm. This was done discreetly with the presence of Witchery Minister as he was the King's keeper. Since Prince Jeff was a baby, the magic and scientific discoveries were too strong for him to bear, therefore some of them were hidden in the heart of the Castle of Goodness. The balance of the magic would be borne by the Prince once he took over the throne.

Prince Jeff inherited the charming characteristics of his father, who had ruled the kingdom for years. As he grew up, his father taught and advised him on what a true ruler should be. Prince Jeff often attended the ruler and chief meetings where decisions were made for the kingdom and built his credibility for years, even at young age. His citizens adored him as he cared for them and was not snobbish.

Prince Jeff was not only exposed to the management of the realm. Witchery Minister taught him scientific inventions for the benefit of the kingdom. Prince Jeff loved science and experiments as he scored A's for those subjects. He was born with a scientific, analytical mind which led him to be interested in developing digital gadgets. He spent most of his time in the laboratory with Witchery Minister whilst other children went out to play in the garden.

When Prince Jeff was only thirteen years old, he developed a transparent travel capsule with the assistance of Witchery Minister. After several failed attempts and many adjustments to the capsule, he used his gift of magic as the final touch, sprinkling it onto the travel capsule. Finally, the capsule was able to enter different dimensions. During his early teenage years, Prince Jeff used the travel capsule to visit different realms without the knowledge of Witchery Minister. He travelled to other planets and got into trouble by not wearing the appropriate clothes as weird temperature existed on different planets. There was no detector on the capsule so Witchery Minister was unable to track his whereabouts in order to bring him to safety.

On his fourteenth birthday, he invented a fountain with magical water for the Queen, who loved fashion and nice scenery. The water in the fountain was spelled to turn into fresh water if the intruder was good-hearted; while the water would turn muddy if the intruder was wicked. He managed to add some magic dust in the diamond-shaped pond—this water changed good-hearted intruders into statues made from the Queen's favourite gem stones, like opals, but changed wicked intruders into black statues.

His latest invention was to bring the travel capsule to Planet Earth. He had heard a lot of stories about Planet Earth and he was excited to visit its nature as well as various human cultures. In addition, on his fifteenth birthday, Witchery Minister and Prince Jeff had started building a detector so that the whereabouts of the travel capsule could be tracked if any incident occurred. However, the detector was still a work in progress.

Unfortunately, his parents went missing in the enchanted forest after their spell went berserk. They were believed to be killed by the Three Weird Sisters in Desperate Valley...

CHAPTER 12

FASHION TO DIE FOR

It all happened in autumn last year, when the King and Queen went for their monthly village rounds. Bloomingflower Road had a mixture of middle- and working-class families. A tailor's shop caught the Queen's eye since she likes to see different types, styles, and patterns of materials as well as the latest fashion. The Queen was in awe of the fashion that the tailor advertised in front of her shop so she stopped and went in. The tailor proudly presented the Queen with the latest dress styles and the colour tone in the Young Magazine.

As the Queen flipped the pages of the magazine, she noticed that the middle page was filled with an empty frame. The title of the page was 'My Queen, My Prisoner'. It was really weird, so the Queen squinted at it, trying to look through the empty page. A gust of wind blew from the page and a whirlpool appeared, sucking the Queen into the magazine. The tailor and the Queen's subjects gasped as the Queen disappeared into thin air in front of their eyes. They looked for the Queen under the chair, in the cupboard, and even under the tailor's working table but were unable to find her.

"Let's trace the sequence of events," the tailor said. "It all started from the wind we felt when the Queen turned to the middle page of the Young Magazine."

The tailor picked up the magazine and turned to the page. To their surprise, the Queen had shrunk and was placed magically in the empty frame on the empty page. They immediately reported the incident to the King.

The King was surprised at the situation. He sat down on the chair and turned to the next page to find any clue on how to release the Queen. At the end of the magazine, there was a riddle:

Sunny sunshine, pungent and decayed air
Thick clouds to blind your vision
This realm is covered with trees with crooked branches
Sharp leaves in olive colour with no flowers
The ground is mostly muddy with insects
Selfish Queen who is so vain.
Colourful fashion to die for.

This is the realm that you need to find to save your dear Queen's life.
Within 48 hours the Queen will die

The King flipped to the middle page to check whether the Queen was alright. The Queen tried to say something, but the King could not hear anything. His Prime Minister said the description in the riddle fits the realm owned by the Three Weird Sisters.

The rescue mission consisted of the King, Witchery Minister, and five security guards. The King told the prince what had happened and to replace him while he is gone. Prince Jeff nodded in agreement. The seven of them went deep into the heart of the castle, underneath the centre of the castle where the King's most powerful magic was kept. They stopped in front of white wall. The King flicked his fingers and a door slid open. The room they entered was empty of everything except a glass cylinder that was in centre of the room. This was the travel capsule that Prince Jeff was working on. The King flicked his fingers three times and all of them were magically transported to Desperate Valley. True enough, they landed on muddy ground with insects flying above it, in a gloomy enchanted forest filled only with trees with crooked branches. This forest didn't have any flowers to beautify its scene.

Witchery Minister marked the spot where they landed, then whispered in the King's ear, "Let me use my magic spell for us to immediately arrive at the Weird Sisters' mansion." He twirled his magic pen in the air and all seven of them landed in the old mansion.

CHAPTER 13

LET THE GAME BEGIN

"Well, well, well. Look who has arrived! The King of the Castle of Goodness who will soon to be our servant!" Danielle laughed wickedly.

The Three Weird Sisters were known for being cold-hearted and remorseless, with the desire to end one's life if rules were not obeyed. They possessed magical powers that could destroy a person in a split second.

"What brings you here?" Danielle asked in a fierce voice.

The King replied, "I came to save the Queen's life. Please undo this magic and I will give you anything you wish for except for my kingdom, wealth, my prince, and the citizens."

"Aaah that is very noble of you, my King. In order for your vain Queen to be freed, all seven of you will be put to two tests. If all succeed, the Queen will live and all of you can return to your kingdom. However, if even one of you fails, the Queen will die and you, the King, will be locked in the dungeon of Desperate Valley forever." Danielle laughed. "Now let the tests begin! Oh yes, I totally forgot to give you the golden rule. No magic can be used. The test environments will freeze your magic."

In a split second, Witchery Minister and three guards found themselves on planet Pluto. Test Number 1 was to see who could endure the coldest temperature for 48 hours without food. Witchery Minister and the three guards planned to stay warm and survive the test by walking, shaking their hands, and huddling together to share body heat. The planet was cold, dark, and empty. Luckily for them, Witchery Minister was born with the ability to see in any kind of darkness. The three guards depended on Witchery Minister for direction. Since they were unable to see in the dark, they stumbled on rocks and their legs frequently sank in the soft sand. Consequently, Witchery Minister had to keep pulling them out of the sand.

Test Number 2 required the King and the remaining two castle guards to survive in the hottest lava of a volcano for 24 hours. They had to prevent themselves from falling into the orange-red lava and to avoid being burnt by the lava that shot up in the air at random intervals. Luckily, the two guards had brought their gilded royal shields. The shields were made of steel, which helped protect them from the lava splash. As their feet were unable to withstand the heat while standing in one spot, the three of them walked from one large black stone to another. Whilst they were jumping onto another black stone, one of the guards lost his balance and fell into the steaming, hot lava.

"Help! Help! It's so hot!" he cried.

The King heard him and abruptly stopped, turned his head to look. He saw the guard sinking into lava.

"Game over, I win," Danielle's voice was heard in both places as though she was using a microphone.

The King pleaded, "Please give us another chance. Name whatever you wish for..."

Danielle's eyes grew big and she smiled widely. She twirled her skinny fingers and muttered a spell. *Poof!* She brought the King, Witchery Minister, and the four remaining guards into her work room at the old mansion. Danielle called Angie. Angie immediately appeared from thin air. They faced each other and held hands. A gusty wind twirled around the room, and poison was released within the magazine holding the Queen captive. The Queen turned blue and froze. She became a picture in the Young Magazine, no longer alive.

The King was so angry that he activated his medal's technological powers. A laser beam shot out from the medal towards Danielle.

Danielle shouted in anger as it burnt her baggy pants. "My pants...you ruined my favourite pants! Her temper rose to the fullest. "I have no remorse for you, King of the Castle of Goodness. I was about to spare your four guards and Witchery Minister's life, however your action has caused me to banish them forever!!"

Danielle placed her skinny fingers in the air. This time, she turned them anti-clockwise and muttered a different spell. The King and his four guards vanished, turned into colourful stained glass windows in a deserted area of the old mansion. They were guarded by a dangerous olive-coloured Tata Duende.

"Tata Duende Eli," called Danielle, "send this message to Prince Jeff: With sadness, we are informing you of the death of your beloved King and Queen and their subjects when their magic went berserk during the Battle of Desperate Valley."

The message reached via the royal official email and it was announced to the Prince. In a rage, the Prince said, "I will protect this kingdom against those three Weird Sisters."

***

Witchery Minister had managed to escape during the commotion of the Queen being turned into a picture in the paper magazine. He whispered to the King that he would go and get help from the castle. The King nodded in agreement. Witchery Minister hid in a nearby cupboard, twirled his magic pen in the air, and vanished into thin air. He arrived safely in the enchanted forest. He quickly took out the detector remote to try to find the travel capsule. It detected a green frog instead of the travel capsule.

"Oh my," the Witchery Minister exclaimed, "let me do the manual way of detecting. Luckily, I left my handkerchief along with a black pebble to mark where we parked the capsule."

Witchery Minister wore his spectacles-shaped magnifying glasses to assist him in his search. As he walked through the muddy ground to search for the capsule, he passed crooked tree after crooked tree for about 30 minutes. He said to himself, "I think I'm going in circles. Let me place a mark to ensure I do not repeat my search in the same place."

So he marked the start of his search journey with his magical pen. As he walked forward, a cricket sat on his head, distracting him. However, the cricket caused Witchery Minister to turn his head to the east. He smiled as he saw his handkerchief and the black pebble beside a huge rock. Without wasting any time, he quickened his steps towards the huge rock with the hope that the travel capsule was still hidden there. To his relief, the travel capsule was undisturbed. Quickly he entered the password for the door to open. He got in and started the engine. The capsule shook slightly. Witchery Minister shivered.

"Oh my, why is this capsule so unstable," Witchery Minister cried out loud.

CHAPTER 14

A SURPRISE REALM

Val and Billy landed in another realm as Val was still learning to control Mother Reddy's magic wand.

"This realm looks like a desert," Val told Billy.

Suddenly, four furious CreulBlocks surrounded Val and Billy. They were creatures with turtle features on a man-like face, and bodies like stocky iguanas. The leader came in front, face to face with Val and Billy.

"What brings you to the realm of the Tagu Tagu?" he demanded.

Val uttered nervously but sweetly, "We accidentally arrived here. We were supposed to land in Desperate Valley."

Joe, the leader of the CreulBlocks, looked in fear when Val mentioned Desperate Valley. "No creature survives in Desperate Valley," he said. "The Three Weird Sisters are some of the most powerful creatures in all the realms. Why do you need to go there?"

"My mother was captured by the Three Weird Sisters while trying to obtain an ingredient to reverse the invisibility spell on Billy's paw," said Val.

Joe looked down at the rabbit's leg and, true enough, it was invisible. "Even though all of us look fearsome, in actual fact we are good in heart. As long as your heart is not wicked, we will allow you to stay here as our visitor until you find the correct spell to take you to Desperate Valley."

Val and Billy were brought to the main hut. A few CreulBlocks sat to the left and right of the main hut while Joe took his seat on the throne.

"Welcome to my lovely guests. Let us help you find the correct spell to reach Desperate Valley," said Joe. "What transportation or instrument brought you to my peaceful realm?"

Val replied that she had pointed the magic wand towards the empty space and uttered a magical spell.

"Maybe the spell I uttered was wrong and led to your realm King Joe," Val replied nicely.

The next day, Val and Billy were escorted to the west part of the realm, where the library was located, to source for the correct spell. Once they arrived, Val and Billy were in awe. The library was huge and full of books. The shelves were made of green jade. Tall pillars trimmed with gold leaf rose up to the ceiling.

King Joe said to Val, "Please make yourself at home. You can search for the book of magic that will assist you to reach the right realm. A librarian will accompany you in this royal library."

Without wasting any time, Val referred to the library index to search for the book. However, it was written in Latin. The librarian came to her rescue by translating it into English. Val went to the first pillar on the right and picked several books on magic. The books were mostly about the magic of farming and friendship, and she could not find any that taught how to reach her destination. After many hours, Val and Billy were tired. One of the CreulBlocks guards escorted them to their guest hut.

"You are cordially invited to a dinner at the main hut," said the escort.

As they entered the main hut, traditional music started to play. Joe was seated on the throne. Dinner was served but

Val and Billy had no appetite. They forced themselves to eat due to the hospitality shown to them. Val showed Joe and the other royal CreulBlocks in attendance her mother's magic wand. Joe recalled seeing this twisted branch and rose design in the Book of Secrets.

"This wand is hereditary. Its magic is strong and can be dangerous if it falls into the wrong hands. If a non-royal CreulBlocks were to possess it, they will become extremely dangerous as the combination between our monstrous self with the strong magic will make our hormones unstable. This can trigger murderous actions in the realm that can lead our realm to extinction. Val, please keep this wand beside you 24 hours and never allow a single CreulBlocks to touch it," said Joe.

Val nodded in agreement.

***

In every realm there is always someone who is naughty, selfish, and has bad intentions. The same was true for Tagu Tagu. A royal CreulBlocks named Jacob had a good friend named John, who was a non-royal CreulBlocks. They grew up together since primary school.

One day, whilst John was visiting Jacob, he overheard a royal CreulBlocks conversation regarding the powerful wand. John was not born rich. His father was a civil servant, working in the administrative department of the kingdom. John's plan had always been to become the Prime Minister in order to influence the King. One of the reasons he maintained a good friendship with a royal CreulBlocks was the hope that he would be able to work in the Royal Circle. For many years, he had tried to enter the Royal Circle but didn't pass the test. It would be the chance of a lifetime for him to own the wand.

After Val and Billy had been there for a week, John started influencing his royal friend on the idea of ruling the realm. Jacob liked the idea of replacing his cousin Joe since his ancestors have been ruling for decades. It was high time for another branch of the royal family to rule the realm. Jacob smiled at this idea.

John said to him, "Once you are on the throne, I will be your Royal Minister, to advice you. We'll conquer lots of realms to make ourselves powerful by possessing their powers. This can be done by being the ruler of the realm." He stroked his beard, dreaming of the intense power he would obtain. As Jacob began to speak, John stopped dreaming.

"Good idea indeed, my dear friend. But how do you plan to get hold of the wand whilst it is guarded by the wretched small kid? Also, we don't even know how to use it once it falls into our hands."

Jacob slammed his right hand on the table nearby in frustration.

"Don't worry, that is something for us to explore," John said with a fishy smile.

CHAPTER 15

RESCUE MISSION

At Val's cottage in Coundonny Don, Coventry, Bob sniffed at the automatic cage beside the wooden work table. He smelt rabbit feet and odour. Bob continued sniffing around the cage to trace the rabbit smell while Ashley used her special auto-ring to track their footprints on the floor. In the midst of searching, Ashley accidentally pushed over a stool.

"Ouch! How rude," said the stool.

Ashley and Bob were surprised at the noise.

"Who is there?" Ashley asked.

The stool kept quiet and still, closing its eyes.

Feeling suspicious, Ashley crept quietly to find the source of the sound. Since she could not comprehend the soft sound that she heard, she continued searching for the footprints. The speaking stool started to follow behind Ashley closely. Ashley saw its shadow and quickly turned her head towards its direction.

"Got you!" Ashley said.

The stool was so startled that it nearly hit Ashley, its eyes wide open.

Surprised by this commotion, Bob accidentally knocked into a medium-sized ceramic vase which had the face of a weird man painted on its front. It smashed to the ground and the ashes inside scattered on the floor. In seconds, the glittery gold ashes combined itself into the shape of a man. Ashley and Bob looked at each other. The man was the one painted on the front of the vase. His face was dark blue, and his eyes were emerald in colour. He had a black moustache and curly hair like spaghetti with meatballs smashed on it.

"Oh yes! I am a free man! I am such an immortal!" he exclaimed. "I would like to thank you both for freeing me." He bowed in Ashley's direction. "I was stuck in that small vase for more than a thousand years."

"Who are you?" Ashley asked.

"Don't you know me? I am the famous Speed Twister."

The old man zoomed past Ashley like a whirlwind, blowing her dark brown hair in all directions. In a split second, he was in front of the locked study door.

"See why I am called Speed Twister?"

Ashley nodded in agreement and smiled. "Why were you transformed into glittery ashes and locked in a vase for more than a thousand years?"

Speed Twister stroked his black moustache. "To answer your question, please let me show you and your furry friend what I do."

In a flash, the old man grabbed Ashley by her waist, then ran towards the automatic cage where Bob was busy sniffing around for footsteps and grabbed him in his strong skinny arms. Ashley tried to free herself by kicking the old man's tummy. Her legs went through his tummy since he was a naughty dead spirit.

"Good girls don't kick old people," the old man said to Ashley. In a flash, they found themselves riding a colourful roller coaster. "We are heading towards the Maze Realm where all your dream toys, puzzles, and games are created. The more the merrier of course!" The old man laughed.

Ashley and Bob hugged each other. They didn't feel good about heading towards the Maze Realm. Once they landed, both were awed to see a variety of toys and games for boys and girls stacked neatly in dusty boxes.

Speed Twister continued, "Let me bring you to the production room where toys, puzzles, and games are made and packed into boxes to be sold during Christmas. Let me tell you the true story about this realm. It is located behind Mother Reddy's Special Room. After the death of my dear daughter Elizabeth, I had a special heart for my niece, Mother Reddy, as she became an orphan at the tender age of twelve. Her parents were killed while they were experimenting with a potion to destroy King Sphere.

"Mother Reddy loved to play with dolls and kitchen toys; she even had parties with her dolls! Her love of toys and puzzles persuaded me to build this realm. It provides something beneficial to mankind. Each of the toys, puzzles, and games are made from a special kid's heart's desire..." The old man laughed wickedly.

"Tell me, Ashley, what toys and games do you like to play with? I will show you to each of their rooms to show you how the toys in my realm are different from the ones on Earth," said Speed Twister.

"Ehmmm I love playing hide and seek, Barbie doll, and monopoly."

"That is good. It seems that kids nowadays love playing with those toys and games that you just mentioned," said Speed Twister. He looked tired as he yawned. "We will continue the Maze Realm tour tomorrow as I am tired. I will show you and your cat a bedroom for you to rest today. Come and follow me to the west wing for guests."

Upon reaching the room, the old man informed Ashley that there were two rules in this realm: not to wander at night in any of the toys, games, or puzzle rooms, known as Maze Rooms; and that guests can only return to their own homes with Speed Twister's permission.

"This room is slightly dusty as it has not been used and cleaned for as long as I was in the vase. Let me call the toy broom from downstairs to clean the room first." He muttered a magic spell and immediately a huge broom appeared in the room and started to clean.

Once done, Ashley and Bob slept on a queen-sized bed with a Victorian comforter to keep them warm at night. The mattress was so comfortable, they both fell fast asleep.

***

When the pendulum clock struck three in the morning, Ashley and Bob heard a voice whispering in their ears, calling them...*let's come down and play, the Maze Realm is not a place to sleep.* Unconsciously, they pushed off the comforter that covered them and wore their shoes. Still in her pyjamas, Ashley opened the door. Ashley and Bob tiptoed down the staircase and walked towards one of the rooms. As Ashley was about to turn the doorknob, the door automatically opened for them as though they were expected.

Ashley and Bob were amazed to find six identical blue doors in the room with a colourful lollipop design on the floor. The floor was painted with red, pitch orange, mint green, yellow mustard, and dark blue circles. Merry-go-round music started playing and both Ashley and Bob had to proceed to a door to exit from the room.

Ashley murmured to herself while her fingers were pointing to the six doors…*Eeny meeny miny mo.* Her fingers stopped at the second door on the left. So, she immediately opened the door and entered the room. Icy water suddenly splashed on herself and Bob. She shuddered in the cold. As she stepped further into the room, more ice-cold water was thrown on her and Bob. Her clothes and her dark brown hair were drenched. Bob's fur was wet. Ashley wanted to turn back but the door had disappeared. They had no choice but to walk further onwards although visibility was poor. Ashley thought of using her auto-ring. She directed it straight ahead and it showed them a door on the right. They walked through water puddles. It was wet and slippery, so they had to hold hands to balance themselves.

Ashley said, "Bracelet, release shelter."

Immediately, a transparent nylon shelter covered Ashley and Bob, preventing a big splash of water from hitting them. With its help, they were able to see where they were going. A few minutes later, they reached a door. Ashley twisted the doorknob and they walked into an empty area with pure white walls.

Again, there were six dark blue doors to choose from. Ashley tried the doorknob nearest to her left, but the door didn't budge. Then, Ashley walked to the door beside it, and placed her ear near to the door to listen for any clues. However, she could hear no sound. Confident that her choice was correct, she pulled the door open. As she and Bob entered the room, dark purple slime came falling from the ceiling...

*Splat... Splat...*was the sound of the slime as it fell on the floor.

Ashley and Bob were caught off-guard. They tried to avoid the slime by hopping from one corner of the floor to another.

Splat...

"Oh my! Purple slime landed on my head!" Ashley cried out.

Ashley tried to wipe away the purple slime from her hair and face. Then Ashley and Bob walked further towards another door. This door was smaller than usual.

As they walked towards the next door, purple, blue, pink and green slime continued hitting their heads. Their movements were hindered by the sticky slime. They had to keep pulling their feet and paws out of the slime before moving forward. Finally, they reached the door.

Ashley said to Bob, "Let's go through this door as there is no other door visible here."

Bob nodded in agreement.

Bob walked through first. Ashley had to squeeze her body in order to go through. Halfway through, the door reduced in size. Ashley was stuck!

"Help! Bob, please help! I can't breathe," said Ashley.

Bob meowed ferociously for help. However, there was no help available.

In a few minutes, the sun rose and all the games stopped, the toys dropping lifeless to the ground. The tricky door grew bigger, and Ashley quickly ran away from it.

"Phew!" sighed Ashley

Ashley and Bob were so tired, they fell fast asleep in their dirty and wet clothing in a small room just after the tricky door.

Speed Twister went to the bedroom where he left Ashley and Bob. He was surprised to find that they were not in the bedroom. "Where are these two brats!" he whispered to himself. So he climbed downstairs to search for them in each Maze Room. Finally, he found them fast asleep in the amusement room, on the carpet that covered the marble floor. He took out his pocket watch and triggered the alarm, 'RRIIINNNG'…waking them up.

"So, someone broke the first golden rule by playing in one of the Maze Realm's Special Rooms," said Speed Twister.

"We are sorry, Mr Speed Twister. We were unaware of our actions," Ashley said.

"I am not pleased with your behaviour. I will give you another chance since you're both creatures from Earth. Let's have breakfast in the dining hall."

Ashley and Bob nodded in agreement. After breakfast, they went to bathe. Ashley looked out the bedroom window, wishing that it would rain and the magical gateway would save them from this Maze Realm. She missed her mother and grandmother.

Suddenly Speed Twister appeared beside her.

"Oh! You startled me!" said Ashley.

"Enough dreaming, little girl. Let's start our work," said Speed Twister in a stern voice.

Ashley's eyes widened. "What do you mean by work? You promised that we are your guests and you would like to show us the Maze Realm."

"Ah yes, I must have forgotten. At my age, I tend to forget. Thank you for reminding me, little girl."

"We much appreciate your kindness in showing us your grand Maze Realm," Ashley replied.

The three of them climbed down the staircase and went towards the Barbie Doll Room. Ashley was so excited to find a variety of rare Barbie dolls in this room. She stopped at each doll to read the label indicating which type of Barbie it was. As she read aloud, each Barbie doll's eyes seemed to come alive, giving Ashley goosebumps.

Reaching the end of the room, the door automatically opened to another Maze Room. This room was for boys and was filled with robots, guns, and water pistols. A majority of them were ancient types of toys.

"The toys that you see are unique toys desired by children for Christmas and other occasions," Speed Twister said.

As their tour drew to end, Speed Twister suggested that Ashley and Bob have dinner then go to bed early since both of them would be required to assist him to revive the Maze Realm the next day.

"I would like to remind you again of the two important rules in this realm: not to wander at night in any of the Maze Rooms, and guests can only return to their own homes with my permission."

They nodded. After dinner they went back to their guest bedroom.

Ashley said to Bob, "How are we going to escape from this realm? I don't seem to see any exit that leads us to Coundonny Don or to our home."

***

Ashley still wasn't sure whether it was the auto-ring's or the bracelet's magic that helped her, but she was able to understand Bob's reply in his cat language. Puzzling over it, she said to herself, "Let me test by removing the ring." As Bob spoke, she could understand him. "Next, let me test by removing the bracelet and wearing the ring, I wonder if I can still understand you, Bob."

Bob nodded and started to meow. Surprisingly, Ashley could still understand Bob.

"For the last test," Ashley said, "I will remove both and see whether I can understand you." She smiled.

Bob meowed once he saw Ashley was not wearing any jewellery.

"Gotcha! I can't understand you without these two magical artefacts." Quickly, Ashley wore both jewellery again, afraid of losing them and the power they gave her.

"Why don't we try to find a way out tonight by searching for the magical gateway in one of the Maze Realm's rooms?" Bob said.

"Let's sleep first and then wake up at one in the morning," Ashley said, setting the table clock alarm, "so we are sure that Speed Twister will be fast asleep."

***

Ashley and Bob were sound asleep when they heard a harsh voice whisper in their ears, calling them...*let's come down and play, the Maze Realm is not a place to sleep*. It was like magic. Mesmerised by the whisper, they walked towards the ajar door in their pyjamas. Luckily for them, the table clock rang, breaking the spell.

Ashley looked at her clothes in disbelief that she was in her pyjamas. She quickly changed to her clothes and grabbed Bob. They crept down the stairs and searched for a door to escape. However, the weird realm didn't have any doors anywhere near the dining room, living room, or tea room.

Soft music whispered in their ears again. This time, it sounded too magical. The magical music managed to place Ashley under a spell, making her walk towards a room. Bob was not affected by the magic so he meowed loudly at Ashley, breaking the spell. She fell on the marble floor.

"Ouch!" Ashley exclaimed. "What happened? Why I am in front of a door?"

Bob told her about the incident. She shivered as she felt this place was creepy. Suddenly the door heading towards one of the Maze Rooms opened. Ashley and Bob were curious to learn whether there was an escape route for them so they started walking towards the room.

Once they entered the room, they felt tremors. Out of the blue, they were in a room full of glass mirrors; left, right, front, and back, even the ceiling and floor was covered with mirrors. Ashley and Bob could only see themselves. The optical illusions made them confused about the next steps they should take. The mirror floor started turning slightly clockwise as they walked. This caused them to feel giddy as well as to fall frequently.

Ashley and Bob closed their eyes, holding hands to navigate way towards the exit. That was another obstacle—there was no door to be found. They felt that they had being moving in circles for a long time. Ashley had an idea. She pointed the finger with the auto-ring to the left, right, and front. A laser beam shot out from the ring and stopped the mirror illusion from operating.

Everything stood still. Ashley and Bob walked further ahead to locate an exit. Whilst walking, they saw a small door above their heads. Ashley touched her bracelet. It grew into a trampoline. She grabbed Bob with her left hand and jumped up. With her right hand, she managed to grab onto the doorknob.

The doorknob was slippery. Ashley's hand slipped and they fell onto the trampoline, bouncing up again. This time, Ashley pushed with her weight and flew up harder. She reached for the doorknob and quickly turned it before gravity pulled her back down. Ashley managed to open the door and eventually both slipped through the door. To their surprise, they reached Speed Twister's bedroom.

Speed Twister was wide awake.

"What is this commotion!" said Speed Twister. "My, oh my, naughty guests, you really went against my first rule of the Maze Realm! I have no choice but to place both of you under detention. You are to work for me by cleaning the whole Maze Realm as well as read the requests from the nasty spoiled brats from Earth."

Suddenly, Ashley and Bob found themselves in a dusty part of the Maze Realm with untidy stacks of boxes, torn papers, and broken dolls scattered on the tables and floor. Whilst cleaning, Ashley kept on reminding Bob to be on a lookout for any exit or opportunity to escape to the garden to find the magical gateway. For hours and hours, they kept busy cleaning the boys' toy room. It was not interesting to Ashley therefore she concentrated on her cleaning duty. As they were about to complete their cleaning task, a robot caught their eyes. It had similar features as the Speed Twister. Ashley slipped the keychain-sized robot into her pocket in case it would be of help later.

As the clock struck six in the evening, Speed Twister came in to check their work. Satisfied with the cleaning, he led them to clean up at their bedroom before heading down for dinner. While they were eating, Speed Twister told them that their duty the next day was to read and separate the letters received from children for their Christmas wish into their respective categories. They were to identify, segregate, and calculate the total number of toys, games, and puzzles required from each department of the Maze Realm.

Ashley and Bob nodded sadly. They were tired and missed home.

Before they got into bed, they looked around the bedroom from one side of the wall to another for any exit. Surprisingly, the window in the room had disappeared. They hugged each other and said a little prayer, hoping that they could escape soon.

***

They slept until midday.

At noon, they started to open and read Christmas letters from children. The old man opened his old computer and started to key in the wishes one by one until he reached the 500th letter. In the letter, the boy wished to have a younger sister for Christmas this year. He threw away the letter in disgust.

"Baby alive doll for him then," Speed Twister laughed.

The room that they were working in grew dark. Ashley pleaded for the old man to allow them to return home. However, the old man told them that as they had broken rule No. 1, they were experiencing payback time.

"You will be freed once the punishment is lifted," said Speed Twister.

They slept soundly until the pendulum clock struck one in the morning. Ashley heard her mum's voice whispering in her ears, "Please come down as I would like to give you hugs and kisses."

Spellbound, Ashley walked towards the staircase. This time, she walked down the corridor until the second last room. The door automatically opened for her. Her heart pounded with eagerness to see her mother's face and be in her arms again.

There was an antique rocking chair in the room, with its back facing Ashley. A lady was sitting on it, her hair tied neatly like Ashley's mother. Delighted, Ashley sat on the lady's lap and hugged her. In a flash, the dark emerald rocking chair started rocking faster than normal. Ashley turned to face the lady, discovering to her horror that it wasn't her mother. The lady dissolved into colourful ashes.

Ashley felt different. To her surprise, her hands and feet were small and the rocking chair looked gigantic. She had shrunk to the size of a Barbie doll.

Ashley was part of them now. The older lady that she had hugged on the rocking chair was the senior chairperson for the Barbie Doll Department. She was able to change into different sizes. All the Barbie family were happily chattering amongst themselves when Ashley was shrunk to their size.

A Day and Night Barbie in a glittering pink party top and a netting skirt approached Ashley.

"You must be the little girl from Earth that we heard a lot about from the other Department."

Ashley nodded and they shook hands. Ashley asked, "Why am I the same size as a Barbie?"

Day and Night Barbie answered, "Because the Maze Realm likes you. The magical powers of the realm changed you into one of us. Also, several days ago, the evil Speed Twister was furious at you for breaking his first golden rule so he cast a spell on you and the cat so that your life will be like ours. However, the spell will break once you leave this realm."

Ashley asked, "How does a human being escape alive from this realm?"

"Thus far there are no success stories to tell. He has brought several kids here before. They all ended up as one of the Maze Realm's items forever." The Day and Night Barbie whispered in Ashley's ear, "For your ears only, once you turn into a Maze Realm item, it is difficult for you to turn back to yourself even if you manage to escape—unless you obtain the glittering twister powder.

The powder is located in Speed Twister's office, though sometimes he carries it with him in the shape of a pen."

Day and Night Barbie smiled at her. "Anyway, the night is still young. Let's get to know each other. Barbie is also your favourite doll, I assume."

The 12 Dancing Princess Barbie came and took Ashley's hand. Ashley's pyjamas magically changed into a pink ball gown as the orchestra started to play. The 12 Dancing Princess Barbie and Ashley danced the night away as all the Barbies, Kens, Skippers, and Chelseas danced together with laughter.

Unknown to them, two eyes watched them dancing, peeping from the ancient portrait hanging on the wall of the Barbie Department. Jealous that the Maze Realm found happiness with Ashley around instead of her, the Maiden pointed her magic fingers at Ashley...

CHAPTER 16

ESCAPADE

Bob woke up in the middle of the night and found that Ashley was missing. He sniffed to find her. His senses directed him to climb downstairs. There, he followed Ashley's scent towards the first Maze Room but it was pitch dark. He was unable to smell Ashley inside, so he went on. He continued to sniff and followed the scent of Ashley's footsteps.

He stopped to open the door of the next Maze Room which was the boys' toy room; soldiers fired their rifles, bombs fell, and helicopters flew above Bob's head. He got irritated and pushed the helicopter away, accidentally breaking the helicopter. The soldiers and commander of the fleet were angry at Bob. They immediately planned to ambush him by throwing ropes around his four paws.

"Arggh!" Bob was quick to realise their plan so he jumped and ran out of the room. In the midst of escaping, he accidentally landed on the soldiers' trucks, tanks, and boat, smashing them to pieces. Panicked, he ran into the next room as the door automatically opened for him to enter.

As sunrise appeared, all the dolls that were alive at night became lifeless. Ashley was left sleeping in her party clothes on the rack full of Barbie dolls in their individual boxes. Bob was about to enter the Barbie doll room when Speed Twister snatched him up.

"Where is the little girl? She is not in her bedroom. She'd better not be mischievous again," said Speed Twister.

"Meow," said Bob, disagreeing with him. "From my magical detector, she is somewhere in the Barbie doll room as she played with her favourite dolls the whole night."

The edges of Speed Twister's moustache shifted to the left. It was pointing to the open cupboards full of wooden racks.

"Owh there she is. She must have met the Maiden of the Maze Realm who shrank her to the size of a Barbie doll. Lucky for her, she was not turned into a Barbie doll." He picked Ashley up and placed her in the pocket of his dark blue velvet jacket. "Let's go into my office so I can change Ashley back to human size," said Speed Twister.

As they walked, his pockets flipped up and down as it was located just above his thigh. This movement woke Ashley up. She was surprised to be surrounded by darkness. She grabbed hold of the pocket wall to ensure her stability, however, the sturdy but soft material caused her to slip. She struggled to get up in the small space of the pocket. Beside her was a light brown handkerchief with the emblem ST and two pens she believed contained glittering twister powder.

"I wonder where I am," Ashley said loudly.

Speed Twister heard her and opened his pocket slightly. He peeped inside and smiled. "You are in my pocket, young girl. We are going to my office to undo the spell so you will return to your normal size."

Upon reaching his office, he took Ashley out of his pocket and placed her on his antique work table.

Bizarre…The table looks similar to the one in dad's study, Ashley thought.

Speed Twister muttered a spell and pointed his long stick in Ashley's direction. A flickering light appeared and Ashley returned to her normal size.

"Oh! Oh!" said Speed Twister, touching the tip of his moustache.

"What happened?" Ashley asked him.

"Please look at yourself in the mirror, my child," said Speed Twister.

Ashley turned to a standing mirror beside the desk. Ashley felt flabbergasted upon seeing herself in the mirror.

"Oh no! I am transparent!" cried Ashley.

"You are actually in the form of a hologram," said Speed Twister. He sighed. "Maybe my spell is not working well after I have been sleeping for a thousand years. I will repair it and transform you to your own self, Ashley. Let's go to my study to check for the right reversal spell."

Ashley suggested to Speed Twister, "Can the Maiden of the Maze Realm reverse the spell she cast on me?"

Speed Twister replied, "It is not an easy task. She is not an ordinary lady with an empathetic heart. She is full of revenge after my departure. All the games, toys, and puzzles in this realm are afraid of her and will abide by her rules in order not to be destroyed."

When they approached his study at the opposite side of the realm, they found that it was guarded by two fierce red wolf robots.

"Owoooo!" they howled.

The red wolves tried to bite Ashley but were unable to since she was a hologram. Speed Twister pointed his stick in the direction of the wolves and turned them into mice. They scampered away. The door was difficult to open as it was guarded by a spell.

"Hahaha." The Maiden of the Maze Realm appeared before them. "You greedy old man, you left us behind for a thousand years, leaving the realm lifeless and without glory. All of us were confident that you were dead and gone forever. Since I was the second most powerful creature in the Maze Realm, I took the privilege of ruling this realm. How dare you suddenly appear and take control of my realm?"

The Maiden was full of rage. Without thinking, she placed two of her palms facing Speed Twister and a powerful force pushed Speed Twister further away from the door. Speed Twister pointed his magic stick at the Maiden's powerful force. Both powers clashed against each other. As the Maiden's magic was more powerful than his, Speed Twister was kicked off and landed splat on the opposite side of the realm. In a flash, Speed Twister came in front of the Maiden. He muttered a magic spell and pointed his stick at the study door.

The door opened but immediately shut again. Then it disappeared into thin air as the Maiden placed a powerful spell on it.

"You will never access the study room which holds your ancient magic spells that I inherited when you were gone!" said Maiden fiercely, her eyes red with anger.

With his quick thinking, Speed Twister cast a protection spell on Ashley and Bob so that the Maiden's magic would not harm them both.

"Argh." The Maiden tried to pull Ashley and Bob to her but was unable to do so as they were protected. "Come to me, Ashley and Bob. I can undo the spell for you. I promise to send you back to Earth," said the Maiden of Maze Realm.

Ashley was caught in the middle as she was unable to determine whom to trust.

Speed Twister pointed his stick at Ashley's and Bob's direction and they were sent into his office.

"I have planned for weeks to turn both of you into the perfect gift for the 500th child's wish. He is my nephew and he will get what he wished for," Speed Twister said.

The Maiden overheard his plan. She placed her palms facing Speed Twister again and her powerful magic pushed Speed Twister to the floor. Immediately, Speed Twister pointed his stick and muttered a magical spell to turn Ashley and Bob into a 'Kaydora Reborn Baby' doll.

The Maiden tried to save Ashley and Bob but Speed Twister was faster than her.

"Hahahaha…This is the moment I have being waiting for, to lock you in a doll forever as I did to the other children who trespassed in Maze Realm. You and the cat will be transported to Earth in this doll as promised."

In a flash, they found themselves in a box at a boy named Mark's house. He was a chubby boy known for spoiling his toys after playing with them twice.

"Uncle Speed Twister gave me a girl doll," Mark said to his mother. "She looks like a real human. She can be the sister that I wished for." He was shocked when Ashley's eyes moved left and right when he opened the box. "This girl doll is unbelievably alive. I will name her Bobby."

He placed Bobby beside his bed when he slept. Ashley planned to escape from the doll's body by using the technology embedded in her auto-ring and the glittering twister powder. She was lucky that she managed to steal one of the glittering twister powder pens when she was in Speed Twister's pocket.

She walked out of the bedroom and down the stairs to the front door. She had to fall down and pretend to be a doll when Mark's mum passed by. Lucky for Ashley, Mark's mum didn't notice her, so Ashley quickly crept towards a small study and sprinkled the glittering powder on her body while pointing the auto-ring from her head to her heels. To her relief, she transformed back into a human being and Bob as a cat. Quietly, they crept towards the entrance to escape.

Once they reached the entrance, Ashley said to Bob, "Let's hope this time the magical gateway will appear and bring us home. I feel like we have been away on this adventure for months."

As she spoke...

Lightning, thunder, and a heavy downpour suddenly started... *splish spash splash.*

A magical light flickered. This time, the colour of their journey into another dimension was greyish black...

CHAPTER 17

PRISONER

Danielle, Angie, and Cindy were furious about the stolen magical hairpin. Since Mother Reddy was unable to move due to the magic, the Weird Sisters came to interrogate her.

"Why are you here to steal my Grandma's hair pin?" asked Angie.

Mother Reddy replied, "Please forgive me, my child. I required the magic possessed by the hairpin to reverse an experimental magic spell where I accidentally made a cute rabbit invisible. Please help the furry rabbit."

"Nonsense! You will pay for your wrong doings!" Danielle shouted at Mother Reddy.

She waved her skinny magic fingers in Mother Reddy's direction. In a flash, Mother found herself held captive in the basement of the mansion. She was lying on a hospital bed in a small room similar to a surgery room.

Her hand was cuffed to the bed by an electronic detector device.

Still furious, Danielle paced back and forth in the study. Her two younger sisters watched her from the living room through the open door.

"Let's fast forward our plan to conquer the Castle of Goodness and the whole Enchanted Garden Realm," said Danielle.

"Why must we conquer the castle while we are happy with this mansion?" Angie asked.

Danielle shook Angie. "Don't you get it? It is the only way for us to be known as the most powerful creatures in all the realms! We need to capture another realm with mysterious events and take over the power in the castle. Look at this rank! At the moment, we've fallen behind to third place. Unbelievable! Witch Z is in second place."

In order for the three sisters to fast forward their plan to enter and conquer the Castle of Goodness, they required Mother Reddy's agreement to be part of them. This was because two magical powers from two different realms are stronger than one.

***

Mother Reddy had grown up as a mischievous witch who liked to experiment with different kinds of spells for fun. For example, in school...

"Kabooshzaaaa...turn the eraser to a frog," said Mother Reddy.

The eraser on her class teacher's table turned into frog, frightening her class teacher as it hopped on the table.

Since she was not from a rich family, most of her spells were used to steal food for survival. She used to cast a spell on farmers so that she was able to teleport their chickens, ducks, and eggs to her house so that her family, which included dear uncle Speed Twister, could have a decent meal.

When she lost her parents and had to live with her dear uncle Speed Twister in the Maze Realm, she found out that magical spells could be used for evil intentions. Her dear uncle used his spells to turn naughty kids into dolls or toys forever. His evil intention was to sell unique toys, games, puzzles, and statues to rich families for wealth. However, Mother Reddy refused to turn to evil but remained as a mischievous witch.

Due to that, Mother Reddy refused to abide by the truce that Danielle put forward.

"I will never be an evil witch…nor follow that disgusting behaviour of yours!!" Mother Reddy shouted.

"I will teach you a lesson for opposing my demands," said Danielle.

Mother Reddy was left a prisoner in the same small room. She was anxious to protect herself from the Weird Sisters' magical spell so she used her drenched dark blue cloak. She muttered a protection spell that she learnt from Uncle Speed Twister. She crouched in the corner of the room to watch for anything sinister. Surprisingly, there was none.

The Three Weird Sisters continued with their plan to conquer the Castle of Goodness Enchanted Garden. They started chanting happily:

> *Our astounding ancient Victorian mansion is standing*
> *tall in the realm of the three beautiful Weird Sisters*
> (They flipped their hair)
> *The ground is mostly muddy with insects*
> *The selfish Queen who is so vain is gone…hahaha*
> *The King came to rescue his love…yucks*
> *Hero is so past tense*
> *It's our turn to strive*

We are strong and united
Together we shall win
Hahaha

The three sisters laughed happily as they planned to conquer the Castle of Goodness and its kingdom after the downfall of their King and Queen.

The next morning, Danielle allowed Mother Reddy to take fresh air by walking freely within the compound of the old Victorian mansion.

"This is too good to be true," said Mother Reddy to herself. "I will try to escape during the morning walk."

When Mother Reddy stepped out of the mansion entrance, she immediately changed into a bird. Her dark blue cloak turned minute to fit her newly-transformed body. She felt she was under a spell as she could only fly within the old mansion. She tried to fly beyond the compound, however, as she crossed the line, an electric circuit shocked her, causing smoke to appear at the tip of her tail.

Danielle laughed loudly upon seeing this from the topmost window in the mansion. Mother Reddy felt sad that she was under the Weird Sister's spell.

After flying to and fro, Mother Reddy was tired. She wanted to enter the mansion to rest, but to her dismay, she was unable to enter the door or the window.

Danielle watched her, laughing ferociously. "You are not done training, Mother Reddy. Please train well without disappointing us."

Surprised with this, Mother Reddy sat on an old antique garden chair thinking of how to break the spell.

"Let me try the spell 'Cashacascascas free me'!" ...Suddenly her beak became rainbow-coloured...*sigh*!

CHAPTER 18

NEW ENCOUNTER

At the Castle of Goodness, Prince Jeff was tossing and turning in his chamber. He jolted awake when he had the scariest dream that a leader could imagine. In his dream, his kingdom was enveloped in orange smoke and a lot of his civilians were missing.

Sweat trickled down Prince Jeff's back. His hands started shaking as his automagic bracelet vibrated, a signal that someone or something had landed in his realm. Quickly, he switched on his powerful drone navigator that was equipped with infrared cameras, GPS, and lasers and sent it to view the surroundings of his castle. At the same time, he alerted his Defence Minister, who quietly sent a few drones throughout their realm to identify any intruders.

The castle grounds were peaceful. While navigating the drones, the Defence Minister saw a small white object flying towards the castle. He alerted Prince Jeff.

"There is a small object approaching the castle, Prince Jeff. I will prepare the castle soldiers," said the Defence Minister. "All soldiers, get ready your ammunition and arc reactor shields!!"

Zoom Zoom Zoom!

A white object entered the Enchanted Garden's air space and flew fast towards the castle grounds. When the object reached the same level as the Karri Trees that surrounded the castle woods, the castle soldiers prepared to shoot the object down with the lasers on their shields. However, Prince Jeff detected his royal emblem on the aircraft and instructed them to hold fire. As the object approached the castle grounds, Prince Jeff's automagic bracelet blinked furiously. The cracking voice of Witchery Minister came in via the radio.

"It's me!" Witchery Minister said. "I am coming in very fast. I am unable to control this travel capsule as all of its controls went bizarre upon entering our realm's space, Your Highness. Keep clear, I will try to land at the edge of the castle woods."

Prince Jeff instructed his castle soldiers to be on guard at the edge of the castle woods for the emergency landing of royal travel capsule.

Witchery Minister had the idea of initiating the travel capsule's protective infra laser beams to reduce the damages caused by the fast impact. Once the travel capsule lowered from the Karri Trees, it moved towards the edge of the castle woods. Smoke trailed from the back engines. Desperate to save his best technology and magic teacher, Prince Jeff activated the magic-infused royal emblem on the middle of his belt to restrain and block the capsule from crashing.

Out of the blue, lightning, thunder, and a heavy downpour appeared over the castle garden. *Splish spash splash!*

Prince Jeff was surprised to witness two different weather within the same radius of his castle. A rainbow-coloured magical light flickered like a hurricane and two figures fell from the sky.

The travel capsule landed hard on a barren land with pebbles. The travel capsule broke into two due to the differences in air pressure upon entering the Goodness Realm. Two of the castle soldiers quickly approached the travel capsule to assist Witchery Minister from the wreckage. He was limping as he came out from the capsule.

Upon placing Witchery Minister on a stretcher, Prince Jeff smiled and said, "Welcome home! I need to rush to another part of my castle grounds as, according to my drone detector, two other objects flew in when you returned."

***

Dizziness enveloped Ashley and Bob as they had a terrible landing on the bushes. Ashley had scratches on her elbow as she had flung her arms wide upon landing. Once they regained consciousness, they could see their surroundings covered with red fern leaves and turquoise Delphinium flower bushes. They had landed in a garden maze which looked similar to the one where they had left Dash as a statue. Bob sniffed around nearby. As Ashley tried to stand, she nearly tripped and fell on the nearby pebbles.

"Ouch!" she exclaimed and sat on the well-trimmed grass looking sad. "Bob, I have tracked the months that we were travelling and, by right, today is my eleventh birthday. Why must an adventure happen on my birthday? I wish I could celebrate with my family instead."

Prince Jeff and four of his soldiers rode their flying scooters towards the neat garden maze. They referred to the Prince's powerful drone navigator to locate the objects that had fallen into the garden maze. Within a few minutes, his drone was able to locate them. Prince Jeff was surprised to see a petite human girl wearing blue clothing and a cat on the drone's screen. As he neared their location, his automagic bracelet vibrated and gave a green signal to signify that the objects were not a threat. Due to that, he signalled for his four soldiers to lower their weapons.

In order not to frighten away the intruders, the five of them left their flying scooters three metres away and crept quietly through the bushes. As Prince Jeff pushed the well-trimmed bushes aside, he suddenly met eye-to-eye with Ashley's almond brown eyes.

Ashley was so surprised that she immediately stood up and grabbed Bob. Upon seeing a well-dressed teenage boy, she smiled.

Prince Jeff was amazed that a young girl had come to his realm via the magical gateway.

Ashley apologised for making a weird entrance to his realm. "We actually wanted to return to our home in Kuala Lumpur. However, we were unable to control the magical gateway once we left the Maze Realm. We landed here instead." Ashley continued to negotiate with Prince Jeff to give them some time to find the correct magical gateway.

Prince Jeff nodded at Ashley's plea.

The four guards accompanied Ashley and Bob to a guest bedroom on the fifth floor on the west side of the castle. After freshening herself, she was instructed to join Prince Jeff for dinner in the royal dining room.

Whilst Ashley was getting ready for dinner, Prince Jeff did a thorough background check on her by referring to his computer and gathering information from his secret agent on Earth. He found out that she is a human being from Earth and Bob is an animal that doesn't harm anyone. Both had been traveling on their adventure for more than a year.

As Ashley entered the dining room, she noticed portraits of the royal family hanging in the air against the wall. Robots served them food. The dining chair looked antique, but had been fitted with electronics. It sensed Ashley approaching and moved out to give her space to sit. Once Ashley sat, the chair moved to adjust Ashley's distance to the dining table.

Whilst having her dinner, she was surprised to notice that one of the royal family's portraits looked similar to her late father. She was staring at that particular painting when she realised that the royal man was wearing the same auto-ring as hers.

The next day after breakfast, Ashley and Bob went out to the garden maze to locate Dash's statue. They went round and round the garden trying to locate the diamond-shaped pond but were unable to find it. Instead, they found fountain with antique silver garden chairs surrounding it.

As Ashley reached out to touch the fountain, her auto-ring started to vibrate. Puzzled, she was about to investigate when Prince Jeff called her. She retraced her steps and walked towards Prince Jeff who was standing a few feet away from her.

"Today, my schedule is to make a surprise visit to my kingdom. Since you are guests in this realm, I would like to personally give you a tour around my realm to introduce you to our culture," said Prince Jeff.

Ashley smiled and nodded in agreement. She managed to whisper to Bob, "Tonight we will investigate these grounds."

***

The tour started outside the castle gates. They rode in flying car with an entourage of royal soldiers. They headed towards the upper middle class residential areas where there were lots of mansions with tennis courts and acres of lawn, some for their pets and others for lawn games.

Next, they visited the city at the end of the realm known as 'Everyone are Friends'. Located further downhill, this city consisted of families from the middle and working classes, who lived together united.

There, they visited the business centres where the office buildings were located. The buildings were capped at 15 floors high for safety reasons, as the community drove flying cars or used electronic transportation.

Once they turned the corner, they approached the shops—small, medium, and huge complexes were visible. Ashley was impressed at how organised and clean this city was. Different parts of the city were designated for living, work, and recreation. This was to ensure that the community's living spaces were separated from the stress of work.

"Cleanliness is the key in this realm. We have robots to clean the streets and pathways, and we repaint our buildings often to ensure the fresh look of this realm. That portrays us as the Realm of Goodness," said Prince Jeff.

As they reached the end of the realm, Prince Jeff and Ashley walked down the river to take in the beautiful nature of the Realm of Goodness. To Ashley's and Bob's surprise, the river flowing in the centre of Everyone are Friends City turned crystal clear and multi-coloured fish jumped to the left and right happily in a welcoming dance. They splashed water on Ashley's cheekbones which made her giggle.

Suddenly, blue, green, and peach-coloured birds chirped and flew above Ashley's head to greet her with lovely song.

> *A pretty girl*
> *From another realm*
> *She is our guest of honour*
> *May she bring our Prince Jeff happiness forever*
> *As her heart is full of kindness.*

Then, all the birds gathered and flew in formation, synchronising to make a heart shape. They repeated their song:

> *May she bring our Prince Jeff happiness forever*
> *As her heart is full of kindness*
> *She is a sweetheart.*

They looked at each other. Ashley blushed and Prince Jeff smiled.

The song was disturbed by Prince Jeff's mobile phone. Prince Jeff received a call from the royal hospital regarding Witchery Minister's condition. Prince Jeff wanted to visit Witchery Minister to gather information about his parents.

"Ashley, my driver will drop me at the royal hospital near the castle. I would like you to proceed to my castle for dinner. Please do not wait for me as I have matters to settle."

Ashley nodded in agreement. She felt tired and she wanted to sleep early.

***

As the clock struck midnight, Ashley and Bob woke up to the sound of voices. They looked out the windows. The sky was royal blue with twinkling stars.

Ashley changed her clothes and crept quietly with Bob towards the back exit of the castle. The door was locked, but to their relief, Ashley's auto-ring released a small sharp pin to unlock the door.

It was pitch dark outside. Ashley used her auto-ring's light function as a torch as they walked quietly towards a fountain. Initially, they thought it was the fountain that they saw in the morning, however, as they approached, they realised that it wasn't. This fountain did not have antique garden chairs surrounding it, instead, it was surrounded by well-trimmed bushes of red and pink roses.

They walked further into the garden maze looking for the fountain with the garden chairs. They went round and round until Ashley tripped and fell. Ashley's auto-ring started to vibrate. Small lights flickered underneath the fountain. Panic struck both Ashley and Bob as royal robotic dogs barked loudly and wildly at them.

Suddenly, the bright lights in the garden maze turned on and castle soldiers appeared with weapons. Ashley and Bob were captured and brought to the Prime Minister's office just outside the castle grounds.

"What do you think you are doing, little girl?" asked the Prime Minister. The Prime Minister was unaware that Ashley and Bob were Prince Jeff's guests as he had been away during their arrival. He thought they were intruders from another realm.

"Guards, place these intruders in our interrogation room now!" he ordered.

Ashley and Bob were locked in a small room with a single metal bed. The room was surrounded with electronic laser bars. They shivered in fear. Ashley tried to think of a way to escape. She threw a steel rod she found in the room at the laser bars in order to see the consequences. The steel rod immediately melted as it passed through the laser bars.

Ashley and Bob were interrogated by the Prime Minister in the morning. The Prime Minister sat in the detention room, asking Ashley for details. However, he didn't believe that Ashley was Prince Jeff's guest.

"He never mentioned that to me," the Prime Minister exclaimed. In order to pressure Ashley to tell the truth, no breakfast was served. The Prime Minister also sentenced them to be hung upside down by their legs for one day.

Ashley felt dizzy. Everything in the detention room was upside down. She closed her eyes. At the same time, she heard Bob meow in pain.

***

When Prince Jeff woke up, he was told by one of his robotic helpers that Ashley and Bob were not in their bedrooms. Quickly, Prince Jeff ordered his royal soldiers to locate them. At the same time, he sent his drone to locate them within the castle's garden maze. However, it was to no avail. The castle soldiers could not find them.

Prince Jeff was desperate to find both Ashley and Bob as they were young and innocent. He was afraid that a mishap might have befallen them. The news that Ashley and Bob were missing spread throughout the castle grounds. One of the royal robotic dogs that caught Ashley last night started to bark furiously. The captain of the royal robotic dogs, who had been on leave the night before, saw its distress and realised that it wanted to show him something. He pressed the playback button on the dog and the recorder showed him what had transpired in his absence.

This information was given to Prince Jeff.

"Royal soldiers! Please get ready my flying car. We need to head to the Prime Minister's office immediately," said Prince Jeff.

Prince Jeff and his royal guards flew quickly to Prime Minister's office. Prince Jeff barged into the office.

"Prime Minister! Release Ashley and the cat immediately! They are my special guests," he cried.

The Prime Minister coughed up the tea that he was drinking.

"Don't tell me you put her in the detention room!" exclaimed Prince Jeff.

He immediately headed to the detention room even though the Prime Minister pleaded for him to stop.

"Let me explain," said the Prime Minister.

The Prime Minister tried to follow Prince Jeff but the prince was too fast for him. He immediately called to his soldiers, "Release Ashley and the cat now!"

In order to release her, they had to reposition Ashley by holding her arms and turning her the right way up again. Then they used a remote to release the laser lock that gripped Ashley's and Bob's limbs tightly.

Prince Jeff reached the room just as Ashley and Bob were released. Ashley looked pale from dizziness, while Bob meowed a lot as he was in pain. Prince Jeff saw their condition and immediately held Ashley's hands and guided her to rest on a chair. As for Bob, one of Prince Jeff's guard carried Bob in his arms.

A few minutes later, Prince Jeff carried Ashley and Bob, who were lethargic, into the flying car which was parked at the entrance. They rushed to the royal hospital located within the castle grounds at the edge of the royal woods. Upon reaching the hospital, Ashley and Bob were placed on stretchers and pushed into the investigation room. The doctor came to attend to them. Ashley's blood pressure, chest, and heart beat were checked thoroughly to ensure that she was completely fine. Luckily for Bob, there was a veterinarian in the hospital that could treat him.

Since Ashley was still a child, the interrogation procedure was too much for her to handle. She was hospitalised for a few days for the doctor to monitor her health and strength. The doctor did some tests to ensure that her overall organs were perfect. Luckily the results of the testing were good. She was only in the state of shock, with her blood pressure increased and her heart beat slowed down due to the interrogation.

While Ashley rested, Prince Jeff took the opportunity to visit Witchery Minister who was hospitalised in the

Ministers' Ward. Witchery Minister was lying in bed recovering from his crash landing. Witchery Minister had injured his right leg badly when the travel capsule broke into two. His leg had to be operated on since debris from the crash entered his skin. In addition, the different level of air pressure when re-entering the Realm of Goodness also caused him to have difficulties with his breathing. The Doctor was monitoring his breathing to ensure it would recover like normal. Prince Jeff was relieved that his breathing was getting better each day.

"I am worried that Witchery Minister is still unconscious. It has been five days already," exclaimed Prince Jeff to the doctor.

CHAPTER 19

NIGHTMARE

Ashley woke up after a nice dream of her mother and late daddy. As she opened her eyes, she could see a drip inserted into her left hand. She was dressed in hospital clothes, and her head felt slightly uneasy. Suddenly, she sat up in her hospital bed as she remembered the interrogation that she and Bob had gone through in the detention room. She looked around the ward but was unable to find Bob. Carefully, she pulled the drip from her left hand. She opened the first door she saw, which turned out to be a toilet. She closed the door and saw another sliding door beside it.

The ward door opened to a brightly lit corridor. The surroundings were quiet, with no one to be seen. She walked down the corridor and read each door signage as she passed by. At the Realm of Goodness almost everything was digital. Ashley was not aware that the doctor had inserted an invisible digital tracker in her arm when she was first warded. This tracker tracked the whereabouts of his patients if they were to wake. Prince

Jeff had also requested the doctor to ensure Ashley's and Bob's safety and full recovery.

As Ashley walked from one ward to another searching for Bob, the doctor was alerted of her movements by the invisible tracking device. He quickly requested a nurse to follow her. Prince Jeff was also alerted as the tracker was set up to send notifications to his mobile. When he saw that Ashley was walking fast around the hospital, he quickly left the official paperwork that he was reading and ran out towards the royal flying car.

Whilst Prince Jeff was on the way to the hospital, Ashley bumped into the veterinarian. The veterinarian recognised Ashley and spoke to her about Bob's condition. Ashley was all smiles as she was relieved that Bob's health was being taken care of. He was also recovering well. Ashley negotiated to visit Bob at the vet hospital that was behind the royal hospital. The vet nodded in agreement as she messaged the doctor to tell him that Ashley was safely with her.

Within a few minutes, Prince Jeff arrived at the royal hospital. He went straight to the vet hospital where Ashley was located. Ashley cuddled and kissed Bob to comfort him that he was safe and would be discharged soon. Prince Jeff saw this and it touched his heart that there is a 'being' from Earth that is good-hearted and well brought up by her parents. Ashley stopped kissing Bob when she noticed Prince Jeff watching her.

Prince Jeff said, "Heard from the veterinarian that you are up and about. I was worried about your health. Do accept our sincere apologies for our Prime Minister's foolish action. It was also my mistake for not informing all my ministers about the arrival of my guests."

Ashley wanted to reply, but her voice was still cracking and just came out as a whisper. Prince Jeff and the veterinarian advised Ashley to return to her ward to continue resting to regain her strength.

As they were returning to Ashley's ward, they passed by Witchery Minister's ward. Prince Jeff looked worried as they passed the ward.

Ashley sensed it and asked, "Who is in that ward?"

"I will let you know once you are tucked in your bed," said Prince Jeff.

Once they reached Ashley's ward and she was tucked in bed, Prince Jeff started to share his childhood journey.

"Please keep whatever I am going to share with you a secret as I trust you as a friend," said Prince Jeff.

Ashley nodded with a smile.

"Witchery Minister is my best friend ever since I was young," Prince Jeff said. "He was with me all the time and was like a playmate, tutor, and an uncle too. I learned a lot from him about developing electronic gadgets from as young as eight. Learning how to utilise and manipulate spells for the use of the realm. I was born with magic and have great interest in science and mathematics.

"My late mother loved trendy fashions and the garden. My father built the beautiful garden maze because of his love for her. I found happiness in the laboratory instead of the garden.

"I will introduce you to Witchery Minister once he wakes up. I am worried as he has been in a coma for a week. I tried using my magic to heal and wake him up, but somehow, I am not gifted with such ability. Anyway, I will let you rest for a while. I will return to visit in the afternoon after finishing the realm's administrative work."

Prince Jeff left and Ashley went back to sleep. Sweet dreams coupled with nightmares jolted her up at four in the afternoon. The doctor and nurse came in to do another round of tests on her. If her results improved, she would be discharged the next day.

After she had dinner, she received good news that she and Bob were fit to be discharged the next day. Prince Jeff received the news when he came to visit both of them after dinner. Bob was placed in Ashley's ward as per Prince Jeff's request. Ashley was cuddling Bob in her arms when the prince came to visit. He smiled and sought permission to pat and brush the cat's fur.

"It feels relaxing and comfortable when stroking cat fur," Prince Jeff said. "We don't have real cats in this realm after a ruthless and greedy tycoon skinned alive all our cats ten years ago. Five greedy tycoons were transferred from Tagu Tagu Realm as they were outcasts. Their body structure since birth was not CreulBlocks creature at all. Since their bodies were similar to the people of Goodness Realm, they had no choice but to stay in Goodness Realm as it is the nearest to Tagu Tagu. It is a myth that a majority of CreulBlocks thirst for cat fur. They believe that cat fur brings them luck. They also eat cat flesh and blood to maintain their sanity and youthfulness. Since these tycoons were born as part of the CreulBlocks clan that was what they did.

"In order to protect the cats, my father the King created a law that no one can own a cat. The law also does not allow cats in this realm. Not to worry, Ashley. Since you are our guests, Bob is free to roam about within the castle grounds. Please stop Bob from wandering out of the castle grounds as he may be caught and given to the Royal Minister of Animals who will eventually transport those cats back to Earth as stray cats."

As they talked, Ashley's auto-ring started to vibrate. "Oh my!" she said.

"What is it? Why is your ring vibrating?" asked Prince Jeff curiously.

"I don't know," said Ashley. "It was a parting gift from my late father. I have yet to further investigate."

As Ashley climbed down from the bed, she shoved her hands in the air towards the wall in front of her ward. The vibrations became stronger, igniting sparkling red lights.

"Let's visit Witchery Minister. He knows a lot about scientific and magical events," said Prince Jeff.

As they were about to leave for Witchery Minister's ward, Ashley placed Bob onto the sofa but Bob clung hard to Ashley's arm, not letting her go.

Ashley carried Bob and whispered in his ear, "Please do not make any sound while we are in the other ward."

The three of them walked quietly towards Witchery Minister's ward. Upon entering the room, they were surprised that the room was extremely cold. They felt like they were in freezer. The bed, sofa, and tables were covered with ice. Prince Jeff quickly took out his mobile to call the doctor and nurses, however, it was so cold that his phone immediately froze. As they stood at the entrance to the room, the door was suddenly bolted behind them. They tried to open the door to call for help but the door disappeared.

The three of them approached Witchery Minister's bed. Witchery Minister was covered in crystal clear ice. It was like he was under a spell as his eyes were yellow and wide open. The trio were about to touch his ice bed when suddenly the ground started shaking. They held on to each other to make a chain so that they would not fall down if the floor were to give way. The ground grew icy. Since it was so slippery, they held hands and walked slowly.

Prince Jeff whispered, "Before someone kidnaps Witchery Minister, let's save him. Let me activate the royal emblem on the middle of my belt. It has a mix of magic and technology that can restrain and block any mysterious power trying to kidnap Witchery Minister."

Prince Jeff activated it and pointed it towards Witchery Minister. Once the technology and magic touched him, the ice started melting and Witchery Minister's eyes returned to its normal black. Prince Jeff shifted his belt and pointed it to the floor. However, the power was too strong. Ashley immediately helped him by pointing her auto-ring towards the floor. The auto-ring released red hot beams that stopped the floor from turning to ice. The room slowly returned to normal.

Prince Jeff and Ashley sighed in relief as they had nearly fallen down due to the slippery condition of the floor. Bob was hugging Ashley tightly when this incident occurred. Suddenly, the door opened and the doctor and nurses rushed in after hearing the commotion and seeing what had happened on the CCTV.

Immediately, they placed Witchery Minister on a stretcher and brought him out to Prince Jeff's flying car. On the way back to the Castle of Goodness, one of the Prince's guards called the head of the robot helpers to ensure that the Deluxe Suite be cleaned and prepared for Witchery Minister's stay. This suite was reserved for visiting royalty from other realms, and was not normally occupied for long.

The specialist doctor and nurse were prevented from following them since Prince Jeff wanted the incident to be investigated.

Prime Minister, you are in charge of the investigation. Please provide another reliable and capable specialist doctor to look after Witchery Minister," said Prince Jeff.

Still furious about the incident, Prince Jeff went straight to his office to figure out what had happened. Once Witchery Minister arrived with his four royal guards, the head royal robotic helper came and brought the royal electronic stretcher. All of them, including Ashley and Bob who had secretly slipped in, entered the secret lift towards the Deluxe Suite. Subsequently, the electronic stretcher moved towards the entrance of the Deluxe Suite.

The Specialist Doctor for the Royal Family appeared and placed Witchery Minister on the bed. Then he placed the drip and checked Witchery Minister's pulse and heartbeat. At the same time, one royal guard was stationed in front of the suite door while another was seated inside the room to protect Witchery Minister. They were to alert the head of security if any suspicious incidents occurred.

***

Ashley peeped in at Witchery Minister. She saw something weird on his right hand, similar to a symbol that she had seen somewhere in the Maze Realm. As she tried to recall where she had seen that symbol before, Prince Jeff appeared with a worried facial expression.

"Your Highness, I would like to share with you the health reports of Witchery Minister," the Specialist Doctor said.

"Please continue," said Prince Jeff.

"His organs are functioning well, but I am unable to identify the cause of Witchery Minister's coma," said the Specialist.

"Do you think that there was mysterious spell placed on him?" asked Prince Jeff.

The Specialist replied, "It's possible. You may consider another magical healing option, Your Highness."

Prince Jeff noticed Ashley and Bob standing in the Deluxe Suite. He guided them towards the door, indicating for them to leave. "Please wait for me. I need to brief my guards about their responsibilities."

After he had given them their orders, he took Ashley and Bob towards the secret lift. They went down to the dining room in silence, deep in thought.

"Let's have dinner and if strength permits, let's find a cure," said Ashley.

During dinner, Ashley caught sight of the royal portraits again. The one hanging in the air near to the wall looked similar to her late father. She asked Prince Jeff about that particular royal family member who wore the same auto-ring as hers.

Prince Jeff replied, "He is our dear uncle Prince Herbert IV who vanished 150 years ago during a war. He was one of the famous royal magical warriors. He possessed a lot of knowledge and magical powers that has enabled Goodness Realm to claim victory against the Three Weird Sisters' parents and Speed Twister.

"The latter nearly captured Goodness Realm with his trick of camouflage and his dirty invention of swindling kids to enter his truck full of clowns. That was how he trapped and kidnapped kids and turned them into dolls. His magic can only make toys from the heart or breath of real kids, either from Goodness Realm or Earth. The dolls look like human beings, which caused the dolls' prices to sky rocket. His market was amongst the filthy rich in Europe and America.

"He even spread his sales to China, Hong Kong, Taiwan, and Korea where a majority of millionaires resided and believed the dolls to be human lookalikes."

Ashley gasped, thinking how super lucky she and Bob had been to escape from Speed Twister.

"The auto-ring must have saved us! I also managed to steal the spell powder from Speedy Twister whilst I was in his pocket. This item saved both of us too," Ashley said.

"There is a little powder left in the pen. I will protect it in case we need to use it in a desperate emergency."

As they were about to bid each other goodnight after dinner, they heard thunder. Lightning could be seen from the window of the castle. Ashley and Bob looked at each other, wondering if this was the magical gateway to return to home that they have been waiting for. To their despair, it lasted momentarily and there was no heavy downpour. They did not see the magical gateway.

Prince Jeff noticed their actions and said, "If you have to leave, please leave. I do not want to be your hindrance."

"The magical gateway didn't appear as expected," Ashley replied, "so we have to stay longer."

Prince nodded and smiled in agreement.

***

As the clock struck two in the morning, Ashley had a vision of a commotion happening in the Deluxe Suite where Witchery Minister was recuperating. She quickly changed her clothes and went to investigate. As she approached the secret lift, she bumped into Prince Jeff who was also in a hurry to check on Witchery Minister. He was startled to see Ashley in front of the lift door.

"Oh Ashley, you are still awake? Why are you hurrying towards the Deluxe Suite?" asked Prince Jeff as they got into the lift.

"I had a nightmare about Witchery Minister and was concerned for his safety," said Ashley.

The Prince said, "Same here, I had nightmare of him being taken by a wicked witch."

Suspiciously, the front door guard was nowhere to be seen. Prince Jeff used his remote control key to open the door. As they entered the room, they could not see the guard stationed in the room either.

Ashley's auto-ring started to vibrate. She looked around cautiously for any surprise movements. As Ashley moved her hands towards the ceiling, the auto-ring vibrated even faster. Ashley looked upwards and saw a guard stuck on the ceiling. Sweat covered his forehead and trickled down on them. His shirt flipped downwards and slightly opened to show his belly.

"Who placed you there?" asked Prince Jeff.

The guard tried to reply but his mouth was missing. Ashley looked twice in disbelief—the guard only had eyes, nose, and ears.

Ashley froze. She recalled a bedtime story her late dad used to tell her when she was seven years old about a girl with the power to save people by utilising her adventure gift. She also remembered the words her dad uttered that the adventure girl would say when things went wrong.

Ashley had yet to explore the other usages of the auto-ring and bracelet, so she decided to use them now. She placed her ring and bracelet facing the ceiling and uttered the same statement as her dad:

Whoosh Whoosh Whoosh
Items of adventure
Over the evil spell we prevail
Make everything normal
Whoosh Whoosh Whoosh

Suddenly, her auto-ring and bracelet lit up with blue rays which enveloped the whole room. The guard fell from the ceiling and his mouth re-appeared on his face. He realised that his mouth has re-appeared which led him to touch his mouth to feel the reality of it.

"Oh my! Where was I?" said the guard in front of the room. He touched his face and body. "I am back to normal!" he exclaimed excitedly. "I disappeared momentarily just now," he added.

Prince Jeff asked, "Guards, did you see anyone entering the room?"

"No, I was sitting on the chair when I suddenly found myself floating in the air and stuck on the ceiling," said the guard who was located inside the room.

"I was about to check the room when I realised I could not see my shoes," said the other guard.

While they were talking and investigating for clues of any intruders, Ashley sat on the chair beside Witchery Minister's bed. As she looked at him, she suddenly envisioned her late dad whispering, "Touch his hands, touch his skin. You will do wonders as you are 'one of a kind'."

Without hesitation, Ashley held Witchery Minister's cold, frail hands in hers. Within minutes, it turned warm. Witchery Minister wriggled his hands.

"Interesting…the symbol on his arm has disappeared," Ashley whispered to herself.

Upon seeing this, Prince Jeff suggested to Ashley, "Please kiss Witchery Minister's forehead to undo the whole spell. It may be just like the fairy tales."

Ashley kissed his forehead. They waited for few minutes but nothing happened. Ashley recalled her late dad's voice. Ashley touched her hands onto Witchery Minister's forehead and the spell was undone. Witchery Minister's hair, face, ears, body and legs turned to normal. He opened his eyes and yawned. Prince Jeff was relieved and hugged him.

"Where am I?" asked Witchery Minister.

CHAPTER 20

BACK HOME

Ashley was amazed that she possessed healing power. She was happy that she managed to save Witchery Minister's life, but she was puzzled about the power.

Prince Jeff introduced Ashley to Witchery Minister, who agreed to fix the travel capsule or build a devise to transport them to Earth and vice versa.

Witchery Minister covered Ashley's and Bob's eyes with a white velvet bandage to ensure that they did not know the way to his secret laboratory. Upon reaching the laboratory, Witchery Minister entered a passcode on the entrance pad. Ashley's sharp ears heard the beeping of the keypad and was able to decipher the passcode, however she kept it a secret. Once they stepped into the laboratory, Prince Jeff took off their blindfolds.

The laboratory consisted of the latest technology and computers, data analytics machines, arithmetic deciphering machines, and electronic ammunition kept in a transparent glass cabinet protected by laser beams.

They showed Ashley the broken travel capsule and ignited the laser beam to investigate the extent of the damage. Witchery Minister started looking for ways to improve and develop the travel capsule to transport them from one realm to another.

As Witchery Minister and Prince Jeff worked on the travel capsule, Ashley and Bob wandered around the laboratory to find something peculiar for them to innovate. As they walked past the electronic gadgets and computers, Bob's butt accidentally pushed the white wall and Bob suddenly disappeared. Ashley had not been concentrating on Bob's whereabouts and was alarmed when Bob was nowhere to be found.

Prince Jeff pointed with his fingers for Ashley to push the wall. Ashley did and she found herself in a huge library. It was full of books neatly placed in racks. There were two computers on two antique wooden tables to source for books and information. Ashley read the listing of books in the computer as she wanted to source for magical gateway openings to Earth.

Tud Tud Tud!

A loud sound could be heard from the laboratory as Witchery Minister and Prince Jeff tried their best to fix the travel capsule for Ashley and Bob to return home.

Ashley was about to grab hold of a book of magical spells when another book with golden trimmings started to shake. Glittering stars appeared dancing in the air, attracting Ashley to grab the book instead.

"Come, girl! Pick me, girl, I am your future," a voice came from the book.

She was about to open the book when Prince Jeff shoved it back on its shelf. Phew!

"Luckily, you didn't open the book," said Prince Jeff. "This book contains evil magic."

With lots of testing, re-building, and re-testing of the improvements, Witchery Minister announced, "The newly-built travel capsule is 75% ready! It will require another week or so for completion for real testing."

Ashley looked happy with this new update.

After dinner, they went to bed early as they planned to start working early on the travel capsule. Ashley also wanted to find a book on electronics and magic to help her control her magic as well as to gather knowledge about the electronic accessories her dad left her.

***

Past midnight, a heavy downpour with lightning and thunder started. A gusty strong wind blew. The numbers on Ashley's ring started to move fast forwards and backwards. Concurrently, her bracelet charm started to make a clashing sound. Bob woke up and meowed loudly in Ashley's ear. She woke up abruptly at the sound.

Bob pointed at the window. Outside, lights flickered at the fountain with the antique silver garden chairs.

Ashley whispered to Bob, "This must be our chance to return home. Let's quickly get ready and head outside."

Within five minutes, they walked downstairs towards the entrance.

Prince Jeff's tracker device alerted him of their movement, waking him up abruptly. Deep in his heart, he knew that the magical gateway that brought Ashley and Bob into his realm existed and he would like to witness it. Quickly, he changed his top and pants and put on his magic belt. He also brought his new Royal Digital Sceptre with him as he felt uneasy with the situation and wanted to protect Ashley and Bob if any mishap occurred.

He alerted Witchery Minister that he was following Ashley out to the garden maze. As Ashley and Bob opened the castle door and walked towards the fountain, someone grabbed hold of her.

"Oh my! Please let me go!" Ashley cried loudly as she struggled to free herself from the grip.

They let go of her, and Ashley turned to see the Prince and Witchery Minister.

"What a relief to see you, Prince Jeff," said Ashley. "My electronic accessories informed me that the wind and rain are the signals of the appearance of the magical gateway. This will lead us back home." She smiled.

"Good luck and may you return to your home safely," said Prince Jeff. "Please take my handkerchief as a token of our friendship. Please treasure it. I hope you will return one day to Goodness Realm to be trained by Witchery Minister to control your magic and the gadgets that you own."

Ashley smiled and took the handkerchief. She kept it safely in the right pocket of her blue dress. Prince Jeff hugged her to bid her farewell. A gust of strong wind blew at that moment, pulling all four of them with its great force.

"Argh! Hold on tight, Witchery Minister! Let's grab hold of the garden chair," said Prince Jeff.

They tried their best not to be swallowed by the whirlwind but their strength was incomparable to the magical gateway of light.

"I am losing my grip, Witchery, let's hold hands so that we are not separated," said Prince Jeff.

All four of them were absorbed into the gateway. This time the gateway was rainbow-coloured.

***

"Arghhh," Ashley cried out loudly and Bob meowed as they crashed landed on Grandma's Delphinium and hibiscus flowers. They scampered on the ground, dizziness enveloping Ashley as she had been on the adventure for more than a year.

Mum and Grandma heard the loud crash noise and ran towards the garden. When they saw Ashley and Bob, they were bewildered.

"Young lady," Mum said, "you are supposed to be in school today. Why are you playing with the cat in my garden?" She folded her arms.

"Mum, I was not playing, I just returned…" said Ashley.

"No more nonsense, Ashley!" Mum interrupted. "Here you go again, with your dreaming adventure!"

Grandma whispered to Ashley, "Did you have fun?" She chuckled. "Please tell me all your adventures later."

As they went into the house, Ashley looked back for Prince Jeff and Witchery Minister. She remembered that they had been sucked into the magical gateway together with them and was worried about them.

"Bob, we better search for both of them since Earth is a foreign realm for them," said Ashley.

Bob nodded in agreement.

Ashley continued, "They would be lost without us to guide them as they would not understand the differences in culture if they were to walk about freely."

Since she missed school, Ashley decided that it was fine for her to linger in the garden.

Ashley and Bob searched high and low amongst Grandma's Delphiniums, bougainvillaeas, and hibiscus flower bushes but they were unable to find any trace of Prince Jeff and Witchery Minister.

"Prince Jeff! Witchery Minister! Where are you?" Ashley shouted.

Still there was no sound from them.

Ashley said to Bob, "Since we have checked the whole garden and we could not find them, let's search for them at the car porch. They must be hiding somewhere."

As they walked towards the car porch where Dad's brown car was parked, Bob stepped on something hard. He stopped and looked down. Under his paw was a wooden doll. Ashley stopped skipping and inspected the wooden doll. It was wearing a fancy top with a 'J' embroidered on it and the same electronic magical belt as Prince Jeff.

Ashley looked around. She found another wooden doll opposite where they found Prince Jeff which had the face, grey hair, and similar shirt to the real Witchery Minister. Quickly, Ashley took the wooden dolls and hid them in her pocket.

"We found them!" said Ashley.

She quickly went into the house to search for her grandmother. As she was heading towards the tea room where her grandmother liked to relax, she passed by a calendar. It indicated that her eleventh birthday would be in a month's time. Her mother had circled the day as a reminder. She stared in disbelief. Time must have stopped when she was away in a different realm. She went to the kitchen and looked for her mother's diary. She flipped the pages and true enough, today was a month away from her birthday.

"Wow! This shows that time at the Goodness Realm is not synchronised with Earth," said Ashley.

Shocked at this finding, Ashley hurried towards Grandma's tea room. Grandma was having her afternoon nap while her favourite song played on the radio.

"Grandma," said Ashley.

Grandma woke up with a smile. "Yes, young lady, I know you were out for an adventure just like your dad. No one knows the secret of the adventure except myself. I accidentally stumbled into your dad and granddad's adventure a few years before you were born, when granddad was alive."

Ashley faced glowed with excitement and she asked, "Grandma, do you know if creatures from different realms would turn into wooden dolls upon entering Earth?"

"Aah…" Grandma tried to recall. "Your dad did mention that those from the Realm of Goodness will turn into dolls. They can be wooden or fluffy just like a teddy bear, dressed in similar outfits as they had on before they entered Earth."

Her mother's antique clock outside the tea room chimed three in the afternoon. An idea struck Ashley. She kissed her grandmother's cheek and rushed upstairs to her father's study.

Upon reaching upstairs, she smelt different types of odour coming from the study. She could not make out what the smell signified, therefore she signalled for Bob to be quiet and stay close to her. Then she turned the doorknob.

A gusty wind pushed Ashley and Bob into the room and the door slammed shut, locking behind them. Ashley fell onto the Persian carpet and the two wooden dolls fell out of her pocket. The dolls shook ferociously on the floor. Within minutes, Prince Jeff and Witchery Minister grew to their normal size.

"Oh my, that was so cramped!" said Prince Jeff.

Ashley gasped in surprise.

They hugged each other in relief that they were both are alive.

"Let me see," said Witchery Minister, scratching his head. "It seems that this room has an electronic magnet or magical power to turn us alive. This is something we have to investigate. I remember well—the magic spell book writes that 'beings' from the Goodness Realm enters Earth at their own risk as it's difficult to survive as a wooden doll for long."

Witchery Minister got up from the floor and started to go through Dad's book rack. Nothing seemed unusual. Then he turned to face the opposite side of the room and saw a small, crooked antique clock on top of a small antique table. There was a mirror in front of it. As he was about to walk towards the small table, someone suddenly tried to turn the doorknob. Luckily, it was locked from the inside so Prince Jeff and Witchery Minister hid in Dad's closet before Ashley opened the door.

Mum came in to check on Ashley as well as to give her gift as a remembrance of her late father. She walked straight to Dad's elegant, mahogany brown antique writing table. She tried to unlock the first drawer with a golden key but she was unable to. After trying several times, Mum gave up and gave the key to Ashley.

"You can take whatever stuff daddy kept in that drawer if you ever manage to open it." Mum smiled. "Let's go to bed. It is late and I am sure you are tired."

Ashley nodded and went to bed. Bob was left in the study as he was fast asleep beside the antique table.

Once the door closed, Prince Jeff and Witchery Minister came out of the cupboard. Witchery Minister went back to the small table corner to inspect the clock. Prince Jeff was curious about the hidden items in the drawer. He went to the antique table and found the key, which Ashley had left on the table.

Apparently, the key was magical. Prince Jeff saw magical dust covering the key. He put it in the keyhole and turned the key. The drawer easily opened for him. As he pulled the drawer open, a bright golden light blinded his vision and woke Bob up. Suddenly, a golden fish net was thrown over them and pulled them into the drawer. The drawer shut and the key fell onto the carpet and rolled underneath the table.

***

Ashley woke up at one in the morning. She remembered that Bob and her guests from Goodness Realm were still in the study. She got up and dressed. Upon entering the room, she expected to see three of them but she only saw Witchery Minister. He looked pale as though he had seen a ghost.

Witchery Minister pointed at the drawer. "That...that drawer...It sucked in Prince Jeff and Bob," he exclaimed.

"I must save them!" Ashley ran towards the drawer.

"Wait!" Witchery Minister pulled her away so that she would not share their fate. "Let us combine our knowledge, gifts, and technology to prepare ourselves to bring them back," he added.

They started to search for a miracle by tapping and touching on the small antique clock. One of Ashley's fingers touched a small hole in the centre of the antique clock. Inspecting the hole, she found a touch pad. Suddenly, the mirror split into two, revealing a door protected by a laser beam. Ashley placed her eyes facing the iris scan pad and the door opened. As they entered the room, the lights automatically switched on.

The room was a fully-equipped laboratory with equipment for all kinds of scientific discovery, including statistical data analytics, biochemistry, chemistry, and physics. It also had a place for detector testing, and to build or interpret research work.

Witchery Minister said to Ashley, "Let's start working." Then he added:

> *Goodness Realm is waiting for us to return*
> *We have to save our loving Prince*
> *Direction, planning, and strategy*
> *Is what should we do*
> *Magic and technology mixed*
> *We will be the strongest*

CHAPTER 21
THIRST FOR POWER

After a month in the Tagu Tagu Realm, Val and Billy were still stuck trying their best to find the spell to transport them to Desperate Valley to save her mother.

One day, Val was trying variety of spells outside the royal library. But instead of being transported, she turned flies to toads, and toads to goats…then to dust. She could not find the correct spell as yet.

"Val and Billy, let me bring you to my house to look for more ancient magic spells," suggested Jacob.

Billy gave Val a nudge to signal for her to be careful. Val was not falling for their trick.

"Jacob and John, please assist me to find the correct magic book in the library since the library is the place to search for books," said Ashley.

Jacob and John looked at each other in disbelief at the request.

"I refuse!" said both Jacob and John, crossing their arms.

"TraTraTra," Val muttered a magic spell which transported them into the library.

Curious, Val and Billy ran to find that Jacob and John had landed upside down in the centre of the library.

"Go and get to work. We don't have all day to waste," said Val.

Their faces were red with anger, blue smoke releasing from their heads, at being tricked by a little girl. The librarian came in their direction and sprayed some water on their heads. They blew themselves dry with their own body heat. Quickly, they got up from the floor and jumped to the second floor to search for the correct magic spell.

By afternoon, Jacob and John reported to Val that they had found a book with magic and spells. Val took the book from them and started to read it. Whilst she read the spell, she accidentally pointed the magic wand at both of them. As they walked away, they transformed into toads then into pangolins which turned a pretty shade of purple, and then finally turned back into themselves. Then it happened all over again.

Val and Billy laughed at this sight.

Val said, "Guess this is not the last we will see them."

Jacob and John were not aware of the magic spell cast on them. They went back to Jacob's residence, deep in conversation about how to grab the wand and use it for their benefit. They began to search via the internet with the intention to study the wand, its power, the usage, and the method to conquer other Realms.

They were so engrossed that they didn't realise the spell placed upon them until after an hour or so. John saw Jacob turn into a toad, then a pangolin then into a purple pangolin, and finally back to himself. The cycle repeated again and again. John stared in disbelief. He slapped his face, hoping it was a dream. As he looked, Jacob changed three times. John pulled himself and Jacob to look at the mirror. To their utter horror, both of them changed in the same phases and animals.

"Arghhhh it must be the girl's doing! I want to slap her face badly," said John.

They ran towards the guest hut. Val and Billy were fast asleep when Jacob and John arrived. Instead of making a fuss, they crept inside to steal the magic wand. The hut was hot during summer, so Val had left the sliding door ajar to let in the night breeze. Jacob and John took the opportunity to sneak into the hut via the sliding door. The magic wand was on the side table beside Val along with her pouch of magic dust. Her pink glitter shoes were under the table.

John grabbed hold of the magic wand. His hands burnt as he touched the wand. "Ouch!" he whispered.

Then his legs suddenly froze as Val muttered a magic spell. Val realised that John was trying to steal the wand. Jacob and John begged Val to undo the magic spell so that they can turned back to normal. Without remorse, Val sent them to Joe for punishment.

Both of them were still under Val's magic spell when they reached Joe's residence.

Joe laughed upon seeing this. "So you have been disturbing our guests. Your punishment is to assist our guests to find the correct spell for them to be transported to Desperate Valley. Both of you will be an experiment item in this activity. Val will undo the magic at her own will."

Upon hearing this, they clenched their fists in anger and snarled at Joe. "How could you do this to us!" they shouted at Joe fiercely.

Joe just smiled and showed them the exit.

The next day, Jacob and John were eager to work with Val. They intended to return to normal and try to steal the magic wand.

They worked and tried to build a good friendship with Val. Val tried all sorts of magic spells with Jacob and John as her guinea pigs and reversed them immediately. After a few days of them being good, Val undid the first spell.

After two weeks, while Val was resting during lunch, she left the magic wand on a computer table in the royal library. John was quick to notice that the wand was unattended.

In order to ensure that Val remained unaware of her missing wand, John placed sleeping powder in Val's and Billy's drinks. After a week of spending time with Val, he had managed to copy some spells in his small book, so he muttered a spell whilst trying to steal the wand. This time there was no burning feeling. Subsequently, he hid it in his pocket and grabbed Jacob by the arm.

"Ow ow, my stomach hurts!" John cried out loud. "Let me rest this afternoon." He acted as if he was sick and they went back to Jacob's residence.

At five in the afternoon, the librarian shook Val and Billy. Groggily, they took their belongings and went back to their hut without realising that the wand was missing.

At Jacob's residence, John took out the wand.

"Let's us conquer Tagu Tagu with this magic wand. No one is brave enough to fight against us in this realm," said John.

"First, we need to be stronger than all the CreulBlocks, hehehee," said John.

They held the wand together and in a split second, they felt something change within their bodies. An enormous power developed within them. Their muscles grew bigger and stronger, and their physique looked bolder. Their voices became hoarser and scarier.

Using the wand and some spells, they transported themselves to the main hut, where Joe sat as the ruler of Tagu Tagu Realm. They sneaked in from behind the main hut and pointed the wand towards the guards inside. The guards bowed to John's command and other guards standing within a two-foot radius were hypnotised into a deep sleep so that they did not fight against John and Jacob.

Inside, Joe was busy discussing with Minister Corner about producing more food for Tagu Tagu. He didn't notice Jacob and John entering the hut until their strong reptile tails slapped Joe and Minister Corner. Joe and the minister flew across the room, falling on the marble floor in the middle of the main hut. *Bang!* He crashed into a glass sculpture.

Jacob punched Minister Corner as he was about to get up from the floor.

John grabbed Joe with his bare hands. Joe struggled to escape, hitting John with his royal sceptre.

"Let go of me!" cried Joe.

John was now so strong that he managed to knock Joe unconscious with a nearby vase while they were struggling. John ordered the guards to place Joe in a cage hanging above the fire.

The royal guards outside heard the commotion and rushed towards the back entrance of the main hut. They came in too late to rescue Joe. Jacob and John created a shield with the magic wand.

"Hahaha! My plan finally worked," said John. "I will be the next royal ruler of Tagu Tagu!"

"Jacob, please sit on the throne," said John.

While Jacob was about to sit, John pointed the magic wand in Jacob's direction, freezing him.

"Oh no! My brother, I didn't mean for this to happen. Hahaha…now I don't have you as the barrier to me being the ruler of Tagu Tagu." He called upon the other royalty to bow before him and make him the ruler of Tagu Tagu.

John ordered his guards to bring Val and Billy to him. Once they appeared in front of John, they were shocked to see the major changes in John's appearance. He looked wicked.

"So, what do you think of my great changes? I feel so powerful that I want to conquer the whole realm!" John shouted happily.

As Val was about to mutter a few spells, John used the wand to shut Val's mouth. Val struggled by stomping her foot on the floor and tried to run. John pointed the wand at Val, however, Val managed to use her magic dust to protect herself and Billy.

Furious, John got up from his royal throne and pointed the wand to undo the protective spell covering both Val and Billy. Once the spell was undone, John quickly pointed the wand at both of them again and muttered a spell that he learnt during his research. Val and Billy's eyes turned ice red and their bodies stiffened like robots as they came under his spell. His guards locked them in a cage a few metres away from the throne.

Once John was acknowledged as the ruler of Tagu Tagu Realm, he melted his best friend Jacob and made him the Minister Advisor. Jacob was glad that he was part of his friend's royal administration. They combined their plan to conquer the realm of Desperate Valley as their readings showed that the realm has lots of treasures like diamonds, rubies, and gold located in the heart of the Weird Sisters' mansion.

"Although the Three Weird Sisters are powerful, we have the magic wand to back us up as well as Val to assist us." John removed the magic spell that he placed upon Val and Billy.

As the spell dispersed, the guards held Val and Billy and brought them to John.

"Val, with your help, we will conquer Desperate Valley and steal their treasures," said John. "We know where your mother is located in Desperate Valley. In exchange for your assistance, you will be reunited with you mother."

"What about my wand?" Val shouted.

"I'll hand it back to you for good once my plan has been accomplished," John replied.

Val was impatient. "I want it now!" she said sternly. At the same time, she muttered a few spells and threw the magic dust towards John's direction with the intention of getting hold of the wand.

John was fast. He placed the magic wand on his head to protect him from the magic dust. "You are a fool and such an impatient girl!"

With the help of the magic wand, Val's mouth was sealed and she was cuffed with a magic cuffs on her hands and legs.

CHAPTER 22

PLANNING

Val tried to talk to John, "Ehmmm Ehmmmm mmmm!" Val's eyes widened with anger.

John released the magic that covered her mouth.

"I will require to use the magic wand for us to be transported to and from Tagu Tagu Realm."

John said, "Since I will be leading the troops, I will keep the wand with me, however, in any desperate and dangerous situation, you are to use it for the safety of our team members."

Val replied, "I agree with this plan."

John continued, "I promise that once our journey is successful, I will return the magic wand to you and your mother. Let's not waste any more time.

"We can be victorious in the conquest with good strategy, team work, and a lot of practice with the magic wand. We need to fix reliable, powerful ammunition and marble balls with hypnotising abilities to keep handy."

In this conquest, Jacob was to be left behind to administer the Tagu Tagu Realm while John was away. Since the group had to keep the numbers to a minimum in order not to be seen by the Weird Sisters, John chose two of his strongest soldiers who were known for victory in a majority of fights before this.

His other soldiers and ammunitions creators spent hours in the royal experiment room developing the strongest and lightest ammunition possible. They intended to bring them to Desperate Valley by hiding them in their backpacks. They also created flying electronic detectors.

In addition, Billy was taught by a master archer how to use a bow and practised aiming the arrow straight at its target. The arrow tip was improvised from steel with sharp barbs.

Practice sessions for Val was to master more magic tricks—mostly to transport them from one area or realm to another, to make themselves invisible, and to create shields against any magic cast at them.

As for John, he discussed their strategy with Jacob. He also tested the stolen wand with the spells that he learnt from the books in the royal library to ensure the spells worked.

Before the day of their conquest, they sent a drone camouflaged as a ladybird into Desperate Valley to scout for any guards or creatures guarding the pathway to the treasure. As the magic dust that enabled the drone to enter Desperate Valley could only last for an hour, the drone had to make a quick overview of the mansion and its gardens, the entrances, and any traps placed by the Weird Sisters or monstrous creatures protecting the mansion.

The drone managed to pass through the crooked pine trees with olive-coloured leaves as well as the entrance, which was guarded by four fierce Tata Duende and a magic iron gate. Within a few minutes, it arrived safely in the garden of the mansion. Then, the drone entered the mansion through the back entrance where the maid was located, passed the ancient ballroom, then by a lovely tea room.

Suddenly, at the entrance of the tea room, a huge creature noticed the drone. The creature growled and started to sniff. Jacob, who was navigating the drone, had missed the creature as it flew past quickly. The creature jumped at the drone, but Jacob was fast enough to manoeuvre the drone away from its paws. The creature snatched at it and Jacob evaded again. The ladybird drone managed to retrace its journey by flying back to the garden with the intention of returning to Tagu Tagu Realm.

In the garden, a fierce, gigantic bird appeared from behind and chased after the drone. It open and shut its sharp beak. Its tail was long and its furry feathers were a mixture of red, blue, and light green. Curiously, the bird wore a small, dark blue cloak over its neck. It started to release fire and smoke in the drone's direction. The tip of the drone was slightly burnt by the fire but it was still able to fly. Suddenly, the huge creature with many eyes came in front of it and slapped the drone.

The drone wobbled as Jacob tried his best to bring it back to their realm. With a smoking tail, the drone struggled against strong resistance at the magic gate as it tried to leave.

Crash! Bang!

The drone crashed in the garden.

"Oh my!" said Jacob. "Look at that! The magic gate surrounding the mansion is so powerful, it is impossible for any creatures to enter or escape alive!" he added, feeling nervous as he bit his fingernails.

John said, "Calm down, everyone! This is the evidence that we definitely require a combination of magic wand and our dear friend Val's magic dust for the success of this journey."

On the day of their conquest, all of them were ready with their magic, ammunition, and tricks. Joe, who was trapped in cage with fire underneath, shouted in rage when he overheard their plan.

"Jacob and John! What insanity are you planning?! Stop it! Stop it!" Joe yelled angrily. "No CreulBlocks has ever survived a confrontation with the Three Weird Sisters. They are very powerful."

Jacob and John ignored his pleading and proceeded as planned.

John, his two guards, Val, and Billy were ready to be transported by Mother Reddy's magic wand.

Val muttered the spell. A magic smoke enveloped them and they disappeared into thin air before appearing just inside the magic gates of the old mansion of Desperate Valley.

"Phew! We are in!"

CHAPTER 23

QUEST FOR TREASURE

In the mansion, the Three Weird Sisters were planning their conquest of the Goodness Realm. With their strong magic, they were able to detect Prince Jeff's and Witchery Minister's absence from the realm. They planned to conquer Goodness Realm when both their strongest defenders were away. It was Danielle, the eldest sister and most cunning and powerful of them, who created the magic gateway and the strong wind that pulled Prince Jeff and Witchery Minister along with Ashley and Bob to Earth.

The Weird Sisters were able to detect their movements by using their magical screen in the shape and size of a photo frame.

"Unbelievable!" cried Danielle. "Prince Jeff and Witchery Minister are alive on Earth! They were supposed to turn into wooden dolls FOREVER!" Her face turned red in anger. "How can we conquer their realm now? They are sure to reach their realm before us!" Danielle stomped her feet on the floor.

"Cool down, my sister," said Cindy. The middle Weird Sister possessed the power to create imaginary worlds. "Let me hinder them from returning to their realm." She pointed her index finger which sparkled with emerald fire. "I will place a magical fear in the study—"

"Guess you will place a certain part of the study into a magical imaginary adventure," interrupted the youngest, Angie.

Danielle asked, "And what is your suggestion? How should we trick Prince Jeff and Witchery Minister?"

Angie smiled mischievously and her eyes twinkled as she told them her plan. "I've been keeping track of Ashley's mother in case we needed to use her to our advantage. She keeps a golden key for a drawer in the study that is full of small electronic gadgets that seemed important to Professor Sprinkler. Let's hypnotise her to give the key to Ashley. Whoever opens the drawer will be sucked into a surprise adventure." Angie laughed. "Our dear Cindy may place the adventure wherever her heart desires."

Cindy was happy to hear that she could be in charge of creating the imaginary adventure. "Ehmmm..." she muttered a spell as she imagined the drawer. *Kaazaaaammmmm* the drawer was enveloped in a magic spell.

***

Prince Jeff and Bob were sucked by the magic drawer into an imaginary adventure world. However, Witchery Minister was left behind in the study. The three Weird Sisters were aware of this as they started their journey to Goodness Realm.

"Let's begin our conquest to rule all the powerful realms and be the No.1 powerful and beautiful rulers in the universe! Hahahahaa..." Danielle cried out with confidence while flipping her blue hair.

Before their journey to Goodness Realm, they made a visit to their realm's sacred place. This was where their ancestors would go to gain strength, courage, and blessings for victory in each battle. It was located in the mountains at the northwest outskirts of Desperate Valley, in the opposite direction from Goodness Realm. Since it was sacred, no one was able to enter via magic. Doing so would cause the guests to lose their power for being disrespectful. Due to that, the three of them could only transport themselves magically to a spot five kilometres away from the sacred place and finish the journey by hiking through bumpy, muddy roads and up steep, rocky slopes.

While climbing the steep slopes, Cindy nearly lost her balance. Luckily, Danielle was observant and managed to save Cindy by grabbing her hood and her hand. Phew!

When the Three Weird Sisters finally reached the sacred place, they muttered a spell and a spirit of their ancestors emerged. The spirit circled the Three Weird Sisters' heads six times and announced, "We wish you lots of strength and fortune for what you seek."

Once the ceremony with their ancestors was completed, the Three Weird Sisters began their conquest.

***

The mansion and its surroundings were quiet. John, Val, Billy, and the two CreulBlocks soldiers had arrived at the right time. However, since they were unaware of this, they were cautious as they crept past the garden. There was a ceramic Tata Duende statue at each corner of the garden with eyes installed with cameras to track visitors. There was also a small lake in the garden in the shape of a bean.

Within ten minutes, they reached the back entrance of the mansion where the maid's room was located. As they passed the ancient ballroom, their detector showed that the treasures were hidden nearby. A short distance away, a musical harp started humming an enchanted song that mesmerized all five of them. They followed the sound of the music towards a red brick tower that was a few hundred steps behind the mansion.

Halfway to the top of tower, Val's lips moved. She took the opportunity to utter a spell.

"Lilililaosh," Val muttered. She was no longer under the enchantment. Realising what had happened, Val sprinkled magic dust on the whole group. "Lilililaosh!"

Everyone stopped and stared at each other in disbelief that they were being distracted by the humming spell.

"Let's return to the original route to the mansion," said John.

Krrrrrrr, the detector device that John was holding whirred.

"There is a signal at the top of this tower showing that a rare treasure is hidden there," said John. "All please proceed as planned to search for the hidden treasures at the back of the mansion. One of my guards and I will go up to check out the rare treasure."

As Val, Billy, and the second CreulBlocks guard returned to the back of the mansion, the fierce, gigantic bird started attacking them with its strong wings and hard beak. As Billy hopped upwards, the bird snatched Billy up with its sharp beak. Its long, firm tail shoved the other three to the edge of the garden, away from the mansion entrance.

"Ouch…" Val exclaimed as her head hit the pebbles on the grass. As she turned her head to look at the huge bird, she saw the red and brown bird wore a small dark blue cloak over its neck. It looked like her mother's. She started screaming her mother's name.

"Mother Reddy, I miss and love you! It's me! Your daughter Val."

The huge bird heard her. Tears dripped from her eyes but she was trapped in the body of this beast, cursed by the Three Weird Sisters since she refused to join forces with them. She flew over them again and threw Billy towards them, then chased after them and signalled for them to return to their own realm. However, the three of them did not comprehend the signal and proceeded with their original plan to steal the hidden treasure within the mansion.

Once they reached the back entrance, they quickly walked past the ancient ballroom. Val's magical intuition was able to detect that there were treasures hidden underneath the ancient ballroom. She directed the other two to follow her lead.

Val pushed open the brown door and entered the ballroom. Then she led them towards a dusty vent along the wall. The signal that Val felt was intense. She used her magic fingers to remove the vent cover. They entered the vent. To their surprise, they found themselves on a winding slide into the basement, landing onto golden money with various types of jewellery, as well as ancient warrior shields.

The guard quickly took out three huge knapsacks to gather the treasures. Val and Billy assisted him by gathering some treasure into their backpacks. Thirty minutes later, Val alerted them to leave as she could sense something fishy. All of them quickly packed. Val took out a rope and muttered a spell to ease their journey back up to the ancient ballroom. In a split second, they were in the ballroom. They searched the room, but the brown door was missing.

Val concentrated to see through the walls. She found two identical doors next to each other, one in purple and the other in magenta. That wasn't the colour of the door they entered through!

"Move aside!" Billy moved forward to assist since he had a pair of long ears. He planned to place his ears behind each door to listen for clues that would let them leave safely. He chose the magenta door first as the dark colour was similar to the antique brown door they entered. He heard roaring and screeching coming from behind the said door. "No! No!" Billy jumped aside and went to the next door to listen. This time there was no sound. He placed his long ears again to double check. Billy was confident that it was safe for them to exit through the purple door.

Val took the lead. She got ready by pointing her magic fingers towards the door in case of any surprises. She opened the door and found it peaceful, so she signalled for them to move out from the ancient ballroom.

***

While the others were in the dusty vent gathering treasures, John and his guard continued climbing the steps towards the top of the tower, curious as to what he would find. At the top of the tower was a tiny door. Magic dust with tiny sunflowers danced through the door, mesmerising them to walk closer and closer. John reached for the doorknob, but before he could touch it, the door opened by itself.

Inside the room was a beautiful harp. A beautiful, young lady with wavy blonde hair was embedded in the harp. She saw them and started to sing, "LaaaLaaaLaaaLaaa" releasing more particles of tiny sunflowers in their direction. As the flowers touched them from head to heels, they transformed into pewter miniatures.

The lady-in-the-harp was the three Weird Sisters' guardian. She turned intruders into similar materials as hers if they had the same greedy nature as the sisters. This was to prevent intruders from stealing from the Three Weird Sisters. The lady-in-the-harp threw the two miniatures out of the tower window with her powers. They landed with a loud thud in the garden, growing until they reached their original sizes.

Val and her group heard the sound and went to look. Seeing the pewter statures, they froze in panic. They required Mother Reddy's magic wand to transport them back to Tagu Tagu Realm but the wand was with John!

Billy started to feel insecure and whispered, "Ashley! Ashley, where are you? We need to be rescued from Desperate Valley." He repeated this three times under his breath, tears rolling down his cheeks. "Help us Ashley, please!"

CHAPTER 24

ESCAPE

At Kuala Lumpur, Ashley was busy gaining knowledge and skills for controlling the two electronic cum magic items that her dad had given her. She was also helping Witchery Minister develop her father's travel machine to allow them to travel between realms every day after school. It took them two weeks to complete the travel machine with the assistance of Witchery Minister's magic and skill. Then, they tested the machine, disappearing only to return to Ashley's house.

In the midst of practicing the new magic tricks that she learnt from Witchery Minister to shield from magic and to turn invisible and reappear, Ashley heard a distress call from Billy.

"What!" Ashley said.

Startled, Witchery Minister bumped the side table, knocking over a rack. A huge, heavy book fell from the rack onto a box with a circular key hole. Ashley had never noticed this box before. She took the box and placed it on the table. Words encrypted on it became visible at her touch.

Ashley read out loud:

> *Only the generation of true heart possesses me with great strength.*
> *Sprinkle with love, sprinkle with heart.*

After she read the words, she realised that the shape of the key hole was similar to the circle charm on her bracelet. She put her bracelet near to the key hole to gauge the accuracy of her hunch. It was perfectly matched so she placed it onto the key hole. It didn't open.

"Oh my! Why can't I burst it open?" wondered Ashley loudly. "I have an idea." She tried again while uttering the statement written on the box. "Only the generation of true heart possesses me with great strength. Sprinkle with love, sprinkle with heart."

Light shone out of the key hole, but the box still remained closed. Ashley tried another way. She held her bracelet's circle charm in the key hole while she placed her left hand on the centre of her heart and read the statement again.

This time, the box started vibrating.

"Look! It's moving," said Ashley excitedly. Magical dust and colourful lights shot out of the box, which grew brighter and brighter until the lid opened.

"Good grief," said Ashley.

"Let's check it out," said Witchery Minister.

A dark blue velvet cloth covered the contents of the box. Curious, Ashley removed the velvet cloth to reveal a small sword. Engraved on the sword were the words:

> *The sword will grow as its beholder, Ashley Sprinkler, grows.*

"Awesome! Your name is written on the sword! This is a miracle," said Witchery Minister. "I am amazed!" He nodded his head while thinking.

"Gee, what are you thinking, Witchery Minister?" Ashley asked as she picked the sword up.

"I wonder what miracle it will bring," said Witchery Minister aloud.

A light emerged from the round diamond in the pommel of the sword. A sudden gust of wind blew Ashley's dark brown hair and she suddenly felt stronger as her muscles developed within her and her face matured.

Witchery Minister was amazed with this new development. "Sprinkler...let me recall the name. In ancient history, your ancestors were great inventors who possessed good magic. Good magic meant to heal and save any beings, regardless of if they were human or creatures from other realms."

Ashley stopped momentarily. She could still hear Billy's cry for help. "Witchery Minister, I can hear a distress call for help from my neighbour's missing rabbit," said Ashley. "It is like he is whispering close to my ear and he is crying."

"Ashley, you should rescue him!" said Witchery Minister.

Without thinking but through her true heart, she uttered the statement:

> *Only the generation of true heart possesses me with great strength.*
> *Sprinkle with love, sprinkle with heart,*
> *Let me be at Desperate Valley's old mansion!*

Ashley vanished into thin air, leaving Witchery Minister to continue developing the travel machine.

***

Ashley appeared at the back entrance of the old mansion. She saw Billy hiding behind a bush in the garden and tiptoed quietly towards him.

Billy was amazed to see Ashley. He rubbed his eyes as he thought he was dreaming. When he opened his eyes again, Ashley was still in front of him. He hugged her, tears of joy running down his fluffy cheeks. From the bush where they were hiding, Val and the CreulBlocks guard introduced themselves to Ashley and relayed the situation.

Ashley whispered, "I am here to rescue all of you. I will bring you to your respective realms as I have the way to do so."

When she saw John and his guard's pewter statues upside down in the centre of the garden, Ashley decided to save them later due to the complicated situation of reversing the spell. The four of them ran towards the back of the mansion, which was surrounded by the deadly magic fence. Whilst they were running, the fierce, gigantic bird came in front of them and blocked their escape with its huge strong wings. The bird opened its beak and started to plead with Val. Only Val and Ashley could understand the message that the bird was conveying.

"My dear daughter Val, I miss you a lot. Please stay, join me and the Three Weird Sisters to conquer the Goodness

Realm. We will be the strongest beings in all the realms ever created."

Val was thunderstruck by her mother's request. All her life, Mother Reddy had never been greedy for power. All she had been taught was mostly about playing tricks with the little magic that they possessed. They were just playful witches, not evil ones. Feeling confused, Val remained with the group.

Seeing this, Ashley took out her sword and muttered the spell to Tagu Tagu Realm. In a flash, the four of them appeared at the main hut of the CreulBlocks.

Jacob was happy to see them. "Oh my! I am glad that you are alive. Where is John? Why is he not here?" asked Jacob with worried expression.

Ashley explained what happened. Upon learning of the ill fate that had befallen his friend John, Jacob looked sad.

"Let's rescue him immediately! What I am going to do to rescue him?" he asked.

"We plan to save him next after we save the community of Goodness Realm. We must combine forces to rescue him," continued Ashley.

Meanwhile, Jacob realised his greediness and decided to release Joe with one condition—that Jacob was to remain the Prime Minister.

The Tagu Tagu guard, Val, and Billy placed the treasures they had taken from Desperate Valley in front of Joe's royal throne.

Joe and Jacob decided to check the value of the treasures. They wanted to sell them and use the money for the development of the Tagu Tagu Realm. They called upon the Finance Minister, an accountant, and a jewellery valuer to start appraising the worth of the stolen treasures. It started with the golden money. When the jewellery valuer touched it, it felt too light. The valuer immediately placed the money on the gold weighing machine and found that the money was not made of gold but of zinc and copper. The valuer continued to check the authenticity of the coins. As he brushed the coin, the numbers indicated on the coin faded.

"What a freak!" he said.

Everyone who witnessed it were astounded and confused.

Joe requested the valuer to continue checking the authenticity of other treasures. The valuer continued checking and everyone was dismayed that all the jewellery were fakes. Jacob was mad since they had sacrificed their lives for nothing. The Three Weird Sisters were indeed cunning creatures.

"Unbelievable! Wait until I get my hands on you," snarled Jacob.

CHAPTER 25

UNEXPECTED

Prince Jeff and Bob hit the bottom of the drawer, landing headfirst in surprisingly soft material with their legs sticking up in the air. They slowly got up in the pitch-dark drawer. After a few minutes, a ray of light came in through the key hole, giving them some light to see by. They looked around and saw huge paper clips, a pen engraved with the name 'Professor Sprinkler', and a diary with lots of mathematical information. They walked a little further and found a variety of electronic gadgets. All of the items were ten times bigger than Prince Jeff and Bob.

Prince Jeff exclaimed, "We have either shrunk or the items have grown bigger. If the latter, we must be in the world of giants."

Curious, they walked further into the drawer. Suddenly, they slipped and fell, sliding as if they were riding a roller coaster. The winding route was about ten metres long.

"My heart feels like exploding," Bob whispered.

Then they ended up on a slippery wheeled barrel. They had no choice but to keep pedalling when they suddenly felt that their shoes were wet. They looked down in dismay to see they were floating in a pool of water, which splashed on their shoes every time they pedalled. Within few minutes, the pool transformed into a water slide causing Prince Jeff and Bob to fall.

Woah!

Luckily for them, they sat on the slide which looped downwards. Both Prince Jeff and Bob cried out loud, "Woah! Arggh!" since the slide ride was fast, faces turning pale. They landed on something soft and bouncy and yellow in colour. It was cold. They jumped off the soft thing, which turned out to be a sponge on someone's kitchen sink.

As they were about to walk to the corner of the sink, the tap turned on, drenching them. Big bubbles formed in the sink as the 'being' washed their plates. Prince Jeff and Bob were covered with soap bubbles and... *Ah Choooooo!* They started to sneeze, causing one of the soap bubbles to grow bigger and float up in the air. As it passed by, they were caught inside the bubble. The wind blew the bubble out the open kitchen window and out to the garden.

"Oh My! This is scary," said Prince Jeff as he looked down at the ground from inside the bubble.

It promptly burst on a sharp nail hidden in the grass.

Prince Jeff and Bob fell into the grass.

"This journey and joyride are sooooo tiring, I wish we could be back at Ashley's grandmother's house," Bob moaned.

As they rested on the grass, they heard a motor running in their direction. They turned their heads and saw two four-wheeled go-karts approaching them. Out of the blue, they grew bigger again, so they could fit on the go-kart seats. Prince Jeff and Bob quickly jumped onto the go-karts to try to escape from the mad journey they were going through. However, they were not aware that the journey was part of the magical trick designed by Cindy.

***

While Prince Jeff and Bob were lost in the adventure space within the drawer and Witchery Minister was concentrating on developing travel machines in Professor Sprinkler's magical laboratory on Earth, the Three Weird Sisters were on the way to conquer Goodness Realm.

They wanted to take the magical and technological powers hidden in the deepest secret of the realm for themselves. All three of them started to use their powers once they were five kilometres away from the sacred place.

CHAPTER 26
PLAN B

Upon reaching the Goodness Realm, a sturdy, gold arch with a gilded stainless-steel gate appeared in front of them. All three of them wore dark hoods to cover themselves. They were ready to enter the Goodness Realm. As they were about to step foot inside the Goodness Realm's big arch entrance…

Boink…

They tried again to go through. However, it was like a spring—all of them were thrown a metre away. Surprised and filled with disbelief, Cindy tried to put her hands through the arch.

"Arggh," she said. "Something…like a power is pushing my hands away."

Danielle started to be annoyed and her face turned tomato-red. She threw a fit by covering her body with particles of dotted grey magic. This magic was built from greed, anger, and revenge. It dissipated as it hit Goodness Realm's shield of love and peace. Danielle shot backwards like a firework to a few kilometres away from the realm. She flew back to the foot of the entrance and instructed her other two sisters to retract their plan until they found a solution.

The Weird Sisters noticed that there were passers-by going in and out of the realm while they were blocked from entering. For safety purposes, Cindy looked into their eyes to erase their memories of seeing them, just in case they had noticed their activities of evil magic and inability to enter the Goodness Realm. Angie took the opportunity to sweet talk one of the women who was about to enter the realm.

"Are you from Goodness Realm? What is your profession?" she asked.

"I'm originally from another realm," the woman replied, "however, due to fate, I married a man from Goodness Realm. We met when he was visiting Honeyland with the previous King. It is a known fact that it is difficult for outsiders, that is, non-community or non-flesh-and-blood, to enter Goodness Realm. Almost no outsiders enter at all! I'm lucky to be married to my husband from

Goodness Realm so I can enter and exit anytime with permission and purpose."

With that knowledge, Cindy looked into her eyes to erase her memory of seeing them.

"We will not give up yet," Danielle said to Cindy and Angie. "Let's pay a visit to our Uncle Speed Twister. His previous wife was from the Goodness Realm. He probably knows the secret for outsiders to enter the realm."

***

With the help of their evil magic, the Three Weird Sisters managed to reach the Maze Realm before darkness appeared. As they were about to open the door to the Maze Realm, the Maiden of the Maze Realm, who was dressed in a peach-coloured dress, appeared in front of them. She held her brown sceptre sideways to prevent the Weird Sisters from entering.

"What is your purpose in coming to my realm?" asked the Maiden of the Maze Realm.

Danielle came forward and said, "We are the nieces of Speed Twister. From our magical detector, he was released from the deadly vase a few months ago. We would like to visit as we dearly miss our uncle."

The Maiden, who knew their connection with Speed Twister, released her sceptre. "I am the new ruler of Maze Realm due to your uncle's departure a thousand years ago. There are two rules of this realm that you need to abide by, that is not to use your evil power in the Maze Realm and not to disturb any of the games, toys, and puzzles in this Realm."

Danielle laughed upon hearing this. "We will definitely obey your command," she said, while she chuckled to her sisters.

Then the Maiden replied, "I saw that." She smiled.

She twisted her hands twice and suddenly, the three Weird Sisters found themselves in Speed Twister's office. He was reading his newspaper and was surprised to see his beautiful nieces right in front of his eyes.

"What brings you here, my beloved nieces?" he asked. "I guess you met the Maiden of the Maze Realm before entering the realm. Did she make your life difficult before entering?"

The three Weird Sisters said, "We met her. She is a pleasant lady. We are here to ask for your guidance and to invite you to join forces with us in our conquest. What can you tell us about her?"

Speed Twister spoke about the Maiden of the Maze Realm who was a soft-hearted woman as she originally came from the Goodness Realm. She was married to Speed Twister in the early years before Speed Twister found hatred and returned to evil magic. His thirst for wealth and greed was what caused their marriage to derail and end. It was the Maiden of the Maze Realm, with the assistance of her family, who had locked the greedy old man in the Greek amphora vase that was guarded by an ancient spirit.

Once his story ended, he said, "So you would like to conquer the Goodness Realm? The realm is mostly guarded by magic and advanced technology where no 'being' from other realm could ever own it." His wicked green eyes opened with frustration. "Let me hear your plan, my clever, witty nieces." He touched his moustache as he spoke.

Danielle quickly took out the map of Goodness Realm and showed him the main arch entrance and the royal pathways to other realms that they could use. Speed Twister started to massage his rusty black-and-blue moustache as he thought of a way to enter the Goodness Realm.

Before he could speak, Danielle said, "We three will be good friends with Aunt Maiden. We will melt her heart further to help the three of us enter Goodness Realm through the arch."

Speed Twister smiled and nodded. "If you don't succeed, another plan of ours is to kidnap and place a spell on one of the Goodness community. Let the 'being' open the magical protected gate for us. Another entrance is the royal pathway which is forbidden to any 'being'. Disastrous consequences will befall us if we choose this."

Speed Twister added that the main strategy in this conquest was to disguise themselves as one of the citizens of Goodness Realm. For preparation, all three of them had to dress up as part of the realm. This led Danielle to wear a wig with stripes of grey hair. She put on a long, greyish-brown working dress and draped an apron over its gypsy skirt. Cindy had to disguise herself as a man, so she snapped her fingers and turned herself into a moustached man with greying black hair wearing dirty-looking faded blue corduroy overalls. Angie disguised herself as a thirteen-year-old girl with black ponytails. She wore a green A-line dress with daisies, a lace-trimmed collar, and button cuffs.

"As for me," Speed Twister said, "I will remain my handsome self with a farm hat to cover my hair. I will lure the community to buy our tasty yet spellbound soup…hahahaaha!"

"What soup?" Angie asked.

"We will see when we get there, my curious, pretty nieces," said Speed Twister while laughing.

Whilst Speed Twister and the Weird Sisters were discussing their strategy, Cindy's nose began to twitch. Her magical fingers retrieved a magic crystal photo frame which showed them the commotion happening in their mansion. They saw the magical evil harp turn John and his guard into pewter and throw them at the heart of the garden. The magic crystal showed their treasures being taken by the Tagu Tagu creatures and Val. It also showed Mother Reddy, the strong, gigantic bird, chasing them and preventing their escape and finally it, showed the sudden appearance of a young girl name Ashley who saved them all using a small sword with a diamond.

The four of them looked at each other.

"So many things happened while we are away," Danielle said. "It is good that we have the evil harp, strong bird, and magical gate to protect our mansion."

Speed Twister asked, "Why do you look calm even though half of your wealth has been stolen by that Tagu Tagu creature?"

Angie replied, "It was my idea to place a camouflage spell on the treasures. The spell has hidden the real treasure deep inside the mansion. The treasures underneath the ancient ballroom are fake. Since I am aware of the latest technology where 'being' of a majority of realm will check the universe's internet, the Tagu Tagu creature must have found the location of the treasure through it. The fake treasures were made of steel—so if it were to be detected by a weak magic, it will be read as real treasures."

Upon hearing this, Speed Twister got up from his seat and clapped his hands. "Marvellous!"

***

Angie tried to befriend and persuade the Maiden of the Maze Realm to follow them for a sightseeing adventure. Sensing Angie's suspicious character, the Maiden kept away from the three Weird Sisters by locking herself in the royal study which was guarded by two fierce red wolves. Angie felt disgusted by her reaction so they had to fall on their second plan, which was to hypnotise someone from the community. This was difficult as the citizens of Goodness Realm seldom left their realm.

The next day, they started their journey and conquest by using their magic. Twisting their wrists transported them one kilometre away from the arch entrance to Goodness Realm. They waited for the Goodness Realm community to emerge. An hour after their arrival, a citizen of the Goodness Realm came out from the entrance and passed by them. He climbed on his electronic bicycle and cycled away as fast as he could when he saw the weird creatures looking at him. He managed to escape before Danielle could hypnotise him.

"Owh, we missed one already. He is too fast for me. What energy does this creature possess?" wondered Danielle.

"Let me try to talk face-to-face with one of the Maiden's family members," said Speed Twister. He placed two skinny, wrinkled fingers beside his head and closed his eyes, concentrating on the older man's face. Then he started communicating. "Please open your house door and walk towards the arch entrance. Hug us and bring us to your house. We are your family," he repeated four times.

All of a sudden, an old man walked through the arch gate.

"Only the weakest fall for my trick," said Speed Twister happily.

The old man came towards Speed Twister. They smiled and hugged each other, then Speed Twister extended his long skinny arms towards his nieces and hugged them concurrently. Initially, the three Weird Sisters were shaken by this action and tried to free themselves.

Speed Twister whispered in Danielle's ear, "Stay close to me to get his magical power to enter the realm."

Hearing this, Danielle pulled Cindy and Angie closer to Speed Twister. They end up hugging both old men. In a split second, all of them entered the Goodness Realm.

The old man was unable to speak but he signalled for them to follow him to his house. Once they entered his house, they noticed that he stayed alone. Danielle executed the plans of conquering the realm by swaying her arms clockwise. Thunder rumbled and rain drizzled on the old man's house, accompanied with slight twister wind. The house changed into a built-in café that sells soup. The logo outside read "Delicious Soup Café". Angie placed the old man under a sleeping spell and locked him in his room.

Danielle added a finishing touch with her magic so that the Goodness community would momentarily forget the existence of the old man and would not be suspicious of their sudden appearance and the opening of a new café.

Speed Twister informed the sisters, "We will sell a magical soup to control the community and make them disappear. This is what we call the level 1 of quiet invasion. I know that Danielle has the capacity to create a slow-release spell...let the community eat the tasty soup, fall ill after eating the second bowl, and two days later, disappear into thin air."

Angie asked her uncle, "Why eat a second bowl instead of making them ill on the first gulp of soup?"

Speed Twister replied, "Because we want them to promote our delicious food to others within the community. If they were to fall ill early, it would tarnish our soup café's image and we will not be able to lure in more customers. Once we have made most of the community disappear, it will be easier for us to conquer the Goodness Realm."

'Bravo!' Danielle clapped her hands at her uncle's genius plan.

The next day, they started their café business. Speed Twister used the wireless speaker to attract customers to eat their soup.

"Carrot soup, tomato soap, and asparagus soup to crave for!" he announced.

Many citizens came to eat. They were surprised that the soup was free for the opening of the café. Word of mouth spread from one person to another, and families spoke good things about the café's soup. They operated the business for three days before they overhead a conversation about a family going missing after returning from the café. Danielle and Speed Twister were happy with the new development.

"Everything is going according to plan," said Speed Twister with a large grin.

CHAPTER 27

RIDE

Upon reaching Ashley's grandmother's house, Val and Billy were introduced to Witchery Minister. Ashley and Billy decided to save their friends, Prince Jeff and Bob, first. Val was emotionally unstable after her experience with her mother so she stayed behind to do more thinking.

Witchery Minister updated Ashley on the progress of the travel machine and its magical ammunition.

"A week more and we can return to the Goodness Realm. Please bring back my prince alive."

Ashley and Billy nodded. They pulled at the drawer but it would not budge. They pulled even harder until Billy fell down beside it. His face was on the floor. As he was getting up, he saw a golden key under the table and reached for it.

Then they used the key to open the drawer and were magically sucked into it. They fell into a garden that was covered with weeds. From afar, they heard a motor running.

Ashley said to Billy, "It sounds like a land mover or a go-kart."

Suddenly, a huge red rooster came from the opposite direction…*Cock a Doodle Doo!* The rooster pecked at their hair and fur.

"Ouch! Ouch!" they exclaimed and started to run away, the flock of chickens chasing them.

A hand grabbed them from the bushes. Ashley nearly shouted for help and tried to bite the fingers but stopped when she saw that it was Prince Jeff. He placed a finger on his mouth to signal them to be quiet. Suddenly, they felt tremors on the ground. They held hands so that they wouldn't be separated if they were transported to a different place.

Suddenly, the land gave way and they sank into the ground.

"Arghhh!" cried Ashley.

Once they reached their new destination, their eyes were blinded by sunlight.

They covered their faces and looked in the opposite direction. To their surprise, they had been relocated to the tip of a ride. A belt locked down on their chests and the Suspended Twin Hammer ride began. The ride swung them upside down then rushed down and up again in the opposite direction, then it stopped for thirty seconds before starting again.

"Oh my! This is too fast!"

Billy and Bob nearly fell off the ride since they were small. They hugged each other to form a bigger mass that the belt could grip tightly.

CHAPTER 28

NEW RULER

In Goodness Realm, the Three Weird Sisters and Speed Twister had managed to make fifty percent of the community disappear. The people were sent to the dungeon in Desperate Valley which was covered with muddy swamp flies and guarded by fierce Tata Duende who did not feed them any meals.

With the reduction of the community, their victory seemed to be nearing. In order to rule the Goodness Realm, the Three Weird Sisters had to conquer the Castle itself, the centre of power and authority. The Weird Sisters changed into their normal attire and headed towards the Castle, leaving Speed Twister to clear the café cum house. A flock of blue, red, and yellow birds descended on their heads and pecked at their hair. Cindy and Angie used their hands to chase them away. Danielle, who was quick-tempered by nature, turned one of the birds into pewter in front of a passer-by. It turned out that the passer-by was a royal guard, who ran to the castle and alerted the Prime Minister.

"There are three witches walking towards the castle. Please stand guard," said the Prime Minister.

The Three Weird Sisters noticed that trouble was about to appear. They made a circle and held hands, igniting their magic. They flew up in the sky and hid amongst the clouds above the castle. They saw royal guards and soldiers forming groups surrounding the castle's garden maze. The water fountains stopped flowing and electronic dogs came out from the castle's administration building, preparing for a battle.

The Three Weird Sisters were all smiles, seeing the preparation of the soldiers and guards. Forming groups made their opportunity to conquer faster as their magic would be able penetrate easier.

"Let the show begin!" cried Danielle.

The Three Weird Sisters held each other's arms in a circle and formed a strong force of magic. Black smoke covered them and made a whirlwind as they descended, dispersing the clouds. The magical whirlwind tried to descend further into the castle grounds but the magic bounced back and hit Danielle's left arm.

"Ouch!" said Danielle in pain. Danielle's left arm was slightly injured.

"Let me heal it," said Angie. She placed her fingers on the open wound and it healed within a few minutes.

Speed Twister witnessed this a metre away from the castle grounds. He placed his fingers to the side of his head and used telepathy to send message to his nieces. "Let's try again with Maze Realm magic. I will do this simultaneously when you start your magic whirlwind."

His nieces agreed and restarted their magic whirlwind. At the count of three, Speed Twister ran around the Castle of Goodness at a speed of 100km/h using his magic pen which was full of magic powder. With their combined forces, their power was strong enough to penetrate and break the shields surrounding the castle grounds. The three Weird Sisters and Speed Twister were finally able to enter the castle grounds.

Upon reaching the ground, Danielle immediately took out her black magic wand that had skeletons with sharp fangs on it. She pointed it at all the royal guards, soldiers, electronic dogs, and helpers and turned them into Tata Duende that bowed to Danielle, the new Queen of Goodness Realm.

The first thing they did to control the administration of the Castle was to ensure that the Prime Minister did not turn into a Tata Duende as Danielle required him as an advisor. However, she sprinkled a little evil magic dust on him to ensure he obeyed her commands. In order to ensure long term ownership of the Goodness Realm, Danielle, Cindy, and Angie stayed at the King's royal administrative tower for their official duties.

On the night of the conquest, all four of them gathered in the dining hall to discuss finding the heart of the magic and the latest invention laboratory. They had to find the most powerful magic hidden in the castle.

"We need to find it quickly!" Danielle cried out loudly.

As they spoke, Danielle switched on the rating monitor. To her surprise, Prince Jeff was currently the most powerful 'being' in the universe of realms. She was disgusted with the rating, since they had just conquered the castle.

"We should have been the most powerful 'being'," cried out Danielle in despair.

"Never mind," said Angie, "the rating will change once we possess the magic."

Danielle snapped her fingers. The Prime Minister appeared in front of them and bowed.

"You are to show us where the most powerful magic is kept and the location of the laboratory," Danielle demanded.

Prime Minister said, "The locations of the magic and laboratory are only known by the King, Prince Jeff, and Witchery Minister."

Danielle was furious and started to punish him until he released the information. It was a waste of time.

***

After their fast and frightening rides, Prince Jeff, Ashley, Bob, and Billy were thrown off from the rides and they landed in another adventure.

Ashley tried to use her sword to escape:

> *Only the generation of true heart possesses me with great strength.*
> *Sprinkle with love, sprinkle with heart*
> *Let us be at Grandma's residence.*

In a flash, they were transported to Grandma's garden. Prince Jeff immediately changed into a wooden doll, which Ashley kept in her dress pocket.

Mother said, "Ashley! Come and help me with the groceries."

Ashley went to help her mother unload the groceries then Ashley, Bob, and Billy ran upstairs towards the study.

As Ashley was about to turn the doorknob, she saw a shimmering light through the keyhole. She pushed the door open. To their bewilderment, a two-person electronic travel machine stood in the study, fully completed.

"Welcome back, Your Highness," said Witchery Minister as Prince Jeff transformed back to himself. "This machine requires your powerful magic to transport us back to Goodness Realm."

Before Prince Jeff touched the travel machine, he told Ashley to use the royal handkerchief if she planned to visit Goodness Realm as that was the only magical entrance allowable for a special friend.

"Let's begin our journey," said Witchery Minister, pulling Prince Jeff to sit in the travel machine. He placed his hands in a control compartment and they vanished.

During the journey towards Goodness Realm, Prince Jeff was drenched with sweat as his magic detector gave him a clue of suspicious activity happening in his realm.

"I sense evil magic," said Prince Jeff.

At this, Witchery Minister advised the Prince to be prepared. "According to our magic electronic detector, our realm has been conquered by the Three Weird Sisters and Speed Twister. However, they have yet to control the magic and the laboratory, which is the central uniqueness of our powerful realm," Witchery Minister said. "In other words, we have to land quietly and turn invisible in order to regain our realm."

As their travel machine approached their realm, they saw the emptiness of their realm. Prince could sense the house-turned-café. In order not to be seen, Witchery Minister camouflaged the machine in the clouds and quietly parked in the sky.

***

While the Prime Minister was talking to Danielle, Cindy, and Speed Twister, Angie noticed a dimly lit narrow corridor at the opposite end of the room. A shining butterfly looked in Angie's direction. Curious, she left her seat and walked towards the butterfly. The butterfly flew deeper into the corridor. Spellbound, Angie followed it closely into the hole and turned into a Swarovski crystal butterfly. It was Witchery Minister's doing, one of his plans to regain their realm.

"Angie, come here quick," said Cindy. After a few minutes, Angie didn't appear.

Sensing something fishy as they could not find Angie in the King's royal administrative room, Danielle, Cindy, and Speed Twister went out to the main entrance. They sensed that Prince Jeff and Witchery Minister had returned to the realm…

***

In order to regain his realm, Prince Jeff was not only required to capture or remove the Three Weird Sisters and Speed Twister, he was also required to remove the evil magic spell that had befallen the Castle of Goodness and retrieve his citizens who were held captive in Desperate Valley.

To do this, he required Ashley's magic sword and her electronic jewellery to combine forces with him. Witchery Minister contacted Ashley with his magic telepathy.

"Ashley, the Three Weird Sisters and Speed Twister have conquered our realm. Help! Help!"

On Earth, Ashley was on the way to school when her golden charm bracelet and the auto-ring started to vibrate. However, Ashley ignored them and proceeded to enter her classes.

Once she reached her science laboratory for class experiment, she heard a faint whisper saying, "We need your help."

Ashley still ignored the whisper as she thought her school friends were playing tricks on her. Suddenly, Witchery Minister's face appeared in her test tube, catching Ashley by surprise.

"We need your help," he repeated.

Witnessing this, Ashley quickly ran out of the class and went home. Bob and Billy quickly followed her into her father's study. She took out the handkerchief Prince Jeff had given her, rubbed it against her hands, and took out her small sword. She uttered:

> *Only the generation of true heart possesses me with great strength.*
> *Sprinkle with love, sprinkle with heart*
> *Let me be with Prince Jeff of Goodness Realm*

Poof!

Ashley appeared beside Prince Jeff in the travel machine.

"Tell me what happened," exclaimed Ashley.

"I can feel evil magic enveloping the Castle and Goodness Realm, eating up the realm's good nature within the grounds. It is trying to turn Goodness Realm to the darkness of greed," said Prince Jeff.

"Let's do this together," they said.

"Both Goodness Realm's and Earth's powers combined are the strongest," interrupted Witchery Minister.

The travel machine descended bit by bit, still camouflaged in clouds in the air space of the Castle. They climbed down and hid amongst the bushes at the centre of the Castle of Goodness's gardens.

"What's that sound?" shouted a Tata Duende, pointing its ammunition at the bushes.

Prince Jeff and Ashley held their breaths.

"Bracelet, release an invisible shield," whispered Ashley.

In the nick of time, they became invisible just as four huge Tata Duende walked into the bushes where they were hiding. The Tata Duende left the site feeling satisfied that there were no creatures lurking within the bushes.

Danielle felt their presence. She quickly appeared at the entrance of the castle along with Cindy.

"Show yourself, Prince Jeff! Are you too cowardly to confront me...your new Queen of the Goodness Realm?" Danielle shrieked.

"I am here! I am the true ruler of Goodness Realm," Prince Jeff shouted in return.

Danielle turned red with anger. "You are wrong! I am your Queen!!" Danielle burst out in anger.

As quick as lightning, Danielle pointed her fingers and released her evil magic in Prince Jeff's direction. At breakneck speed, Ashley raised her arm in his direction as well, her bracelet turning into a shield to protect Prince Jeff. Simultaneously, the royal emblem in the middle of Prince Jeff's belt released his good-hearted magic that shoved away the evil magic. Danielle stumbled backwards and landed on the floor. Ouch!

"Arrgh," cried Danielle angrily.

"Stop!" said Cindy to Danielle. "I will play tricks on them by concealing this castle with our mansion in Desperate Valley. This way, they will think they are defeated."

Danielle's eyes twinkled at this plan.

While they were fighting in front of the Castle entrance, Witchery Minister handled Speed Twister in Prince Jeff's study.

"Hi there...It has been a long time since I have seen you," chuckled Witchery Minister to Speed Twister.

"Give me your magic! You have nowhere to go but to bow to us as your new ruler," said Speed Twister.

Witchery Minister was hiding in one of the bookshelves while his hologram was in front tricking Speed Twister. His hologram stood behind Speed Twister and whispered close to his ears, "Never!"

Speed Twister immediately turned and tried to grab hold of Witchery Minister but the hologram disappeared. "I will catch you, you sleazy old man!"

The hologram jumped onto a big antique table and stood on it, shouting, "Come and get me!"

Speed Twister jumped onto the table and lost his balance as he only managed to step on the tip of the table. He fell onto the floor. "Ouch!" said Speed Twister.

He reached into his pocket and took out his magic pen. Witchery Minister saw this from his hiding place and pointed his index finger with magic. *Puff!* The magic pen vanished.

"What?" Speed Twister cried.

Speed Twister was about to take out another magic pen but Witchery Minister distracted him.

Crash...a glass statue fell and shattered on the floor.

Speed Twister ran towards it, confident that Witchery Minister was hiding there. As he reached the spot, he heard Witchery Minister whispering from behind the King and Queen's portrait on the wall.

"You are nothing but a greedy old man," said Witchery Minister's voice from beyond the wall.

Speed Twister placed his hands on the portrait. Behind the portrait, the wall opened widely and a strong wind blew. Speed Twister screamed as the wall swallowed him into the opening of the huge pewter vase camouflaged by the wall. Speed Twister was finally trapped in there.

***

Outside, thick black clouds gathered. Cindy's evil magic was turning the castle into their old mansion, similar to the one in Desperate Valley.

Witnessing this, Prince Jeff gasped in disbelief. "My castle! My kind hearted magic and technology are gone with it," Prince Jeff said in dismay. He dropped to his knees on the ground.

"Give up already and bow to me as your Queen," shouted Danielle.

Ashley tapped on Prince Jeff shoulder. "Don't give up and never bow!" she said.

Then Ashley pointed her auto-ring towards the castle and true enough, the original Castle of Goodness stood steadfast behind the old mansion.

"They are using their evil power to camouflage the original castle," whispered Ashley.

Hearing this, Prince Jeff got up from the ground and with the assistance of his electronic scooter, he managed to appear in front of Danielle instantly. Ashley was not fast enough to stop Prince Jeff's impromptu decision to fight against Danielle himself.

Seeing Prince Jeff approaching them, Danielle and Cindy held their hands together and released their evil magic at Prince Jeff as they chanted their evil magic spell.

Prince Jeff managed to avoid the spell, though it hit his scooter. Prince Jeff flew off his burning scooter. Seeing this, Ashley said "Bracelet, release net!" A safety net came out just in time for Prince Jeff to fall onto it.

Ashley's feelings were hurt that her good friend had nearly met with fatal accident. Furious with Danielle and Cindy, she held her sword above her head and muttered a spell:

> *Only the generation of true heart possesses me with great strength.*
> *Sprinkle with love, sprinkle with heart*
> *Give me the utmost magic to eliminate the evil witches*

As she spoke, bright rays of purple and pink lights enveloped the sky just above her. Her brown hair curled, growing stripes of dark pink. Her face was covered with a pink filigree mask with rhinestones. In addition, her sword's pommel shone with white and blue light which consisted of powerful good magic.

"Awesome!" cried Prince Jeff. "Let's save Goodness Realm!!"

He took out his Sword of Goodness and touched it against Ashley's sword.

They pointed their swords at the Castle. The combination of both realm's power and energy of being true and love for the community brought them freedom from the evil power that had enveloped the Castle of Goodness. The black clouds and smoke dissipated, and the old mansion that camouflaged the Castle vanished.

Danielle and Cindy watched in horror. They tried to escape but were stuck in the compound of the Castle.

Ashley pointed her powerful sword in their direction and magic cuffs encircled both their hands and legs. She twisted her sword back and forth and uttered:

Only the generation of true heart possesses me with great strength.
Sprinkle with love, sprinkle with heart
Let me bring the Three Weird Sisters back to Desperate Valley.

In a split second, Ashley, Prince Jeff, Danielle, and Cindy found themselves at the old mansion in Desperate Valley.

Prince Jeff demanded that Danielle and Cindy release the Goodness Realm citizens that had been tricked and held captive.

At first, they hesitated. Ashley tightened the grip of their cuffs, strangling them.

"Where is Angie? I demand for her to be released," shouted Danielle. "I will release your pathetic citizens once you return our sister Angie!"

Ashley made eye contact with Prince Jeff. He nodded for Angie to be released.

In a split second, Ashley twirled her sword and Angie immediately appeared beside Danielle. She was no longer in the form of crystal.

As Danielle was about to break the spell for the people of Goodness Realm to return to normal, the huge creature with many eyes jumped onto Prince Jeff from behind the back door.

"Ouch! You wild beast, get off from me!" shouted Prince Jeff.

Ashley shoved her sword towards the huge creature, turning it into ice sculpture. Concurrently, concerned that Danielle may pull a trick, she also froze Danielle by pointing her auto-ring at her.

Danielle struggled to be set free and pleaded to Ashley, "I promise to behave and return your people to normal, please unfreeze me."

With that, Ashley unfroze Danielle but left the handcuffs on her hands. Danielle uttered a magic spell to release the people of Goodness Realm who had been captured. They were returned to their own realm as the evil magic spell broke.

Ashley and Prince Jeff combined their swords above their heads and a light came out from their sword towards the old mansion. They uttered a spell:

> *The Three Weird Sisters will be kept as prisoners in their own Realm until they have a change of heart.*

Both Ashley and Prince Jeff returned to Goodness Realm. The prince ensured that all his citizens had returned and were in good health. They cheered for Prince Jeff, Ashley, and Witchery Minister, celebrating their bravery, courage, and their love for them.

"Goodbye and see you again for more adventure, Prince Jeff and Witchery Minister," said Ashley.

Back on Earth in her grandmother's house, Ashley, Bob and Billy looked at the sky over the Kuala Lumpur Twin Towers and wished to save Dash.

The wind blew strongly, they sky turned darkness, with thunder and lightning. A magical light and whirlpool appeared in the garden…

Owh no!

ABOUT THE AUTHOR

Sherlina Idid studied in Coventry University, United Kingdom and graduated with a BA Hons in International Relations & Politics. She has been working in the human resource management line.

Her interest in travelling has led her to be exposed to other cultures, environments, and sightseeing which eventually sparked her to write her first novel. She can be reached on @sherlinaididauthor on Instagram and as Sherry Ina on facebook.